Nika Rising

by

D J Walker

Book Two of the Tek & Nika Series

D J Walker
P.O. Box 145
Sloansville, NY 12160
U.S.A.

paperback ISBN 979-8-9874553-2-6
ebook ISBN 979-8-9874553-3-3

December 2022

Tek & Nika Series ~ speaking of shapeshifters ~
Book 1 – Sliver Of Evil
Book 2 – Nika Rising
Book 3 – Sinuous Passages

Chapter 1

(Book Two begins in prehistoric times, in the northeastern forests of what is now the United States of America.)

The scent of bear drenched the air that Tek breathed. He was in his lynx shape, just barely alive, wedged between a cold earthen wall, and the warm back of a large sleeping bear.

He could do nothing but endure when he was conscious, listening to the bear's hibernal breathing. Pain spiked in his wounds whenever the bear, shifting in its sleep, ground him against the wall.

He remembered who he was. He was one of the People. No longer a boy and not yet a man, he was one of the few among the People who could shapeshift.

He remembered being in his buck shape as he followed Okat in her chipmunk shape through the dark snowy knat, certain she was up to no good.

He remembered Woqri's spirit guiding him . . .

Ani's hysterical cries . . .

S'Kaw as hawk summoning the other shapeshifters . . .

Okat charging toward him in her lethal panther shape . . .

His hooves coming up to fend her off . . .

But his hooves changed rapidly through to his hands and then for the first time ever, into the paws of a small lynx.

In that instant he understood the real meaning of the strange dreams he'd been having: his new shape was *not* a small prey animal, as he had feared it would be. It was lynx. The small animals in his dreams were *all lynx prey*.

The realization immediately followed, that even as a lynx he stood no chance against Okat as panther.

Time yawed between explosive movement and a brutish, dreamlike crawl. Tek felt Woqri insert herself like a wedge between him and the charging panther, enough for him to twist alongside the panther and sink his claws into its back, while hooking his teeth into its shoulder. The slight advantage was brief. The panther shook him off and bit into his neck. With its longer legs and its larger and more powerful claws, it ripped at his chest and gut.

He fought back like a whirlwind. With a crazed savagery he used his claws and teeth and lightning–fast reflexes to fight the bigger cat. The panther would win, but he would use this shape that the spirits had given him in this last possible moment, to wound the panther as much as he could.

Another lynx joined him in the battle, and he caught S'kaw's scent in the second lynx. S'kaw was larger and heavier than he was, and she went immediately for the panther's most vulnerable parts. The panther loosened its hold on Tek to fight back; Tek broke free and used his claws and teeth against the panther to better effect. The three of them rolled and twisted in a frenzied blur of raking claw and gouging tooth.

Fast as the panther was, the two lynxes were faster. They used this and their weight against the panther's longer reach, and its greater size and strength. Reflexively they worked together to throw off the panther's aim and weaken its holds. But the panther still tore and bit deep wounds into them in the wild melee.

The two lynxes tried to grip along the panther's back and flanks, to be clear of its gnashing teeth, and to hobble its legs and claws. The panther kept dislodging them in powerful twists and rolls, until they both got a firm grip at the same time, enough for a brief, slowing respite.

In that moment, while the panther braced to throw them off yet again, the spirit Woqri dropped and held them still a few moments. Tek had just sensed Woqri's purpose when, with a heavy jolt, Woq in his wolf shape charged in and got his jaws clamped onto the panther's head.

The panther threw itself around with renewed fury. Tek, too weakened to risk a bold move, worked his teeth and claws in deeper, and twisted and writhed to throw off the panther's aim and balance.

S'kaw fought savagely with rapid, gouging punctures between the panther's ribs, and clawed blurringly fast, ever deeper into its gut.

The panther clawed back cruelly with manic strength whenever it could free its shoulder or femur from S'Kaw's grip.

Woq as wolf was flipped and flung and rolled over. But with his jaws locked on the panther's head, he was spared from being bitten, while the furious fighting kept up by the two lynxes spared him from being lethally mauled by the panther.

Tek felt the panther weaken. He smelled more of its blood as it slowed and coughed heavily, bloodily. The terrible battle was nearing its end.

When the panther staggered, there was no doubt that it was dying. Tek released his hold and dropped away.

He lost his awareness of S'kaw and Woq, and of almost everything else. He remembered staggering a few steps, before keeling over on the bloodied snow. Every part of him was lacerated, punctured and bleeding, and as he took those last steps, he was aware that lengths of his torn gut trailed the ground.

Then — nothingness. Nothingness until he woke up in the sleeping bear's den — thirsty, hungry, and too weak to move.

He lay there, thinking, remembering.

Many times he relived the desperate battle in the snow — every rip of claw through fur and flesh, every pierce of tooth along bone and into thew.

He also ranged back over his life before the battle. He relived his childhood, including the fateful day when the panther wind's daughter destroyed the knat of his birth and killed his parents. He remembered deciding with his brother Sho to stay and help the knat in its time of need, and the hard, desperate work of surviving that first winter, and then of building the knat in a new place.

He remembered when, at age fourteen, he went with his brother to the Ochwah knat for the first time. He remembered meeting S'Kaw there and the drubbing she gave him. He remembered his brother's wedding feast, and Tsihi — beloved Tsihi.

He wondered at S'Kaw being able to shapeshift into both a hawk and a lynx, and his own surprising lynx shape. He hoped that somehow S'Kaw survived the battle. He did not really think that she had — but then, hadn't he somehow survived it? So it was possible . . .

He thought as little as possible about Okat — about her many shapes, her implacable evil, the sheltered position she had in the knat until her mother died, and the many deaths she caused afterward.

When he was not awake time passed as a blank, except for jumbled, hazy dreams that, as he recollected them, were in two connected series. In the first, he dreamed in a disjointed way of a large scentless bear picking him up from the bloodied snow and carrying him through the woods and deep into a cave, where it poked and prodded at his chest and bleeding entrails with its long, curving black claws. In those dreams Tek was often outside his body, observing the bear as it used the dull rounded tips of its claws with amazing dexterity. When the bear finished poking and prodding his flesh, it coated the bloody loops of his intestines with a foul–smelling paste, and it painstakingly stuffed his entrails back into their lacerated sac. The same kind of paste was mashed into his puncture wounds, and smeared over the tears in his lynx pelt. Toward the end of this series of dreams Tek dreamt that the noxious paste coated nearly all of him, from the lacerations on his nose to the gouges on the tip of his tail.

The second series of dreams seemed like dreams within dreams. He kept dreaming of awakening to a droning chant and the smell of burning herbs. He could not be certain, but over the reek of the paste smeared all over him, the herbs seemed similar to a mix of átia[1] and kastá[2]. Later, when there was less of the foul–smelling paste, the herbs smelled more like anennò:ron[3]. Though he could barely breathe the harsh smoke, his lungs craved it, and he struggled to get as much of it into himself as he could.

The droning chant was one he had never heard the like of before. Over and over, a deep voice cracking with age droned words Tek did not know, though some of them sounded similar to words in the language of the People. At first the voice was soothing, but in the later dreams it sang more brusquely, seeming to exhort Tek to contribute in some way to the healing work. He resisted. Everything

---

[1] similar to sage

[2] similar to cedar bark

[3] similar to sweetflag

hurt, and he had no idea what he was supposed to do. And everything was pointless, because he was certain he was dying anyway.

But the voice grew in urgency, until he could not avoid it by slipping away into either a miasma of smoke, or an empty oblivion. Harried, he began to slowly sheathe and unsheathe his torn and broken claws. It was agonizing, but at least when he made this exertion the voice became less insistent.

From limbering his claws he moved on to tensing and relaxing other muscles, beginning with his paws and legs and working his way up to his torso and neck. The voice prodded him at times, but for the most part he kept up the work enough to placate it.

Several times he tried to shape shift back into a boy, but he could never do it. He was stuck with being a lynx.

*   *   *

Not long after the second series of dreams ended, Tek felt the sleeping bear stirring, awakening. Unlike the scentless bear in his dreams, this sleeping bear was a real one. The confined space of its den was redolent with its scent.

Tek had become used to being lulled by the bear's deep breathing in its sleep. Often it and the wind howling outside the den seemed to merge into the strange chanting of his dreams. But Tek was certain that when this bear woke up, it was *not* going to be pleased to find him in its den.

When the bear roused enough to realize that there was something in its den that did not belong there, it rapidly went from a deep sleep to a full attack readiness.

A bear's sense of smell is among the keenest. This bear knew that there was a lynx in its den, and that the lynx also smelled strangely both of bear and of the two leggers who sometimes hunted it. Lynx and two–legger scents in its den?! With surprised grunts and a sudden violent movement in the confined space, the bear twisted itself around and let out a deafening roar.

Tek was too weak to do anything more than make small, feeble movements. He stilled even those, when the bear roared. Escape was impossible. He waited, resigned, for the bear to eat him.

5

When Tek made no movement, the bear proceeded to sniff him all over very slowly and carefully. When it finished with his exposed side it nudged him over with its snout and thoroughly sniffed the rest of him.

Tek still expected the bear to eat him, but more time passed and the bear did not. It sniffed him all over a few more times, and then — very oddly — it left him alone, as if he wasn't there at all. It went back to sleep for a while, and then got up and lumbered out of its den. When it returned after a short while it did not go fully back to sleep. It dozed, shifting restlessly, grunting as if it was uncomfortable and could not settle down.

During its restlessness the bear continually mashed Tek up against the rounded wall of the den, until he let out a lynx cry of pain, though it was such a weak, feeble sound — unlike that of any lynx he had ever heard. But in response the bear stilled itself and then shifted a little further away from Tek.

Tek knew by the bear's scent that it was a she–bear, and that she was pregnant. He supposed that all of her lumbrous fidgeting was because she was about to give birth.

Before much more time passed, the bear birthed a cub. In the darkness Tek could not see it, but he could smell and hear it. From the rustling sounds it made in the dried leaves of the bear's bedding, it was quite small. But it was loud, and it cried out incessantly from the moment of its birth, while it scraped and squirmed to reach and stay close to the warmth of its mother. Its mother licked it off and continued to roll and shift around restlessly in the cramped den. Soon a second cub was born and the den reverberated with the combined bawlings of both newborn cubs. Finally their urgent noise stopped abruptly and Tek listened thirstily to their suckling, and then to their quiet mews of contentedness. This was followed for a while by the mother bear's deep breathing and the howling wind, before the cycle of frantic bawling, avid suckling and sleep repeated itself. Again and again.

In this den with the self–contained threesome, Tek wasted away, slipping in and out of consciousness. He was most awake when the cubs were bawling, simply because their cries were so piercing and elemental.

Those nerve–grating cries . . . Tek began to notice that with each cycle the noise made by one of the cubs gained in volume and strength, while the other's weakened. In the darkness he heard the mother bear chuffing at and nudging the weaker cub more and more often. The weaker one died not long after that.

The mother bear ate it. In the dead of winter, nothing could be wasted.

It made Tek wonder again why the bear had not eaten him when she first woke up and found him in her den. She would have derived more sustenance from him *then*, than she would *now*. He was getting weaker, closer and closer to death.

But then the mother bear did something unexpected. After the next time she suckled her remaining cub, she swept up Tek's limp body and jammed his head against one of her teats. Some of her precious milk trickled into his mouth and down his throat.

So warm, so rich and sweet! So life giving! Tek struggled to get as much mother's milk as he could. Then he slept, and while he slept a modicum of strength returned to him.

When the mother bear next nursed her remaining cub, she did not sweep Tek up to her breast afterward. Tek lay still for a little while, waiting hopefully, but when nothing happened he began to yelp and bawl in the same way that he had heard the cubs doing. He squalled as robustly as possible, though the effort rapidly drained the precious strength he had gained. When he was nearly exhausted it worked: the mother bear pulled him to her roughly and he was allowed to have some of her milk — more this time. Thereafter whenever the cub cried for milk Tek bawled lustily too.

Slowly Tek gained the ability to move himself to the breast for the milk, though the mother always let her cub finish before she allowed Tek to suckle.

Tek slowly gained strength. The cub — a male — grew in size and became playful with Tek. He humored it, limbering his muscles by rolling and battling around with the cub. But the cub's play was rough. Tek was relieved when at length the winds howling outside of the den lessened, and the cub became distracted by the warmer air reaching in from outside, carrying tantalizing odors. When its mother began to leave the den daily to forage, the cub tried to follow her out.

It was very persistent, and getting stronger. Its mother had to bat it back into the den more and more harshly, before blocking most the den's entrance with snow.

Tek thought maybe he should worm his way out of the den and leave while the mother was gone on one of her forays, but in the end he decided to wait until it was warmer, when he would have a better chance of surviving outside. In the meantime, he tried to keep the cub occupied while its mother was gone.

Occasionally he tried to shapeshift back into a boy, but he could never do it.

When the cub was a little larger, about half of Tek's size as a scrawny lynx, the mother bear let her cub go outside with her for the first time.

That same morning, the mother bear did not let Tek suckle. When he persisted in bawling for her milk, she gave him a hard swat and growled at him. He understood her: he would no longer get any milk from her. He kept quiet after that, thinking about her refusal, until she and her cub left the den. He decided to find another place to live. For if the mother bear turned on him fully, it would be dangerous to be anywhere near her and her cub.

Close to the den's entrance, the mother bear showed her cub how to climb a tree. The cub was willing to learn at first, but it soon tired of the climbing lesson in the midst of all the wonderful scents that it wanted to follow. The mother kept her cub at the lesson though, with a persistence that the cub could not yet understand. When she was at last satisfied, she grunted at her exuberant cub, to follow her away from the den.

Tek came fully out of the den after they left. He judged that it was already well into the Strawberry Moon[4] since the trees and bushes were well leafed out.

Nothing about the area was familiar to him. Nor was there anything that smelled of the People. The only thing he was certain of, from the type of growth around him, was that the den was fairly high up in a mountain forest.

---

[4] June, usually

Tek sat in a glow of sunlight near the front of the den, letting the sun ease the stiffness of his bones. A life–warm fawn breeze ruffled through his fur, and slid along the delicate sensors in his nose. He reveled in his ability to scent so much in the wonderful air. But even as he savored it, he knew that the air and almost all of the scents it carried were not the same as what he remembered.

The mother and cub had gone down a rough path that sloped downward from the den. Tek guessed that it led to a stream and, being thirsty, he got up to follow it too. At the stream he would keep a safe distance from the bear and her cub, and then strike out on his own.

He had not gone far when the wafting breeze brought the scent of wolf on it — the scent of several wolves further down the slope from him.

Tek instantly knew that the wolves were after the cub, and that the mother bear, being too far upwind of the wolves, would not yet know that they were following her and stalking her cub. Wolves being here, so close, could not be a coincidence: they had almost certainly been in the area for days, waiting upwind of the den, for this first outing of the cub with its mother.

It only took Tek another moment to decide what to do. He would have died if the mother bear had not suckled him. Now he would try to repay her by warning her of the wolves.

Chapter 2

Tek raced down the path with as much silence as possible, until he scented the wolves more strongly — four of them ahead of him, loping down the path. Coming up behind them, he veered off the path where it curved sideways to follow a gentler slope. Abandoning stealth, he plunged nearly straight down a steep incline, crashing through brush and sliding, rolling through leaves and tumbling through ripping brambles.

The path wound back around below the slope he was on, so he dropped down onto the path in a near free–fall, off the shoulder of a large boulder that jutted above the upslope side of the path. He landed hard, momentarily knocking the breath out of him.

The lead wolf was just a little higher up on the path. It was a large male, in its prime. Tek saw surprise and a moment of uncertainty flicker in its eyes. He did not wait to see what would inevitably follow — the resolve to attack. He spun away from the wolf, digging his claws into the path and stretching his limbs to their utmost, in an all–out race to reach the bear and her cub before the wolves.

Tek was fast, but the wolves soon gained on him. The deep running huff of the lead wolf got closer and closer. Then the path straightened and widened, and there was brightness through the trees ahead — probably a meadow clearing or the stream itself.

Another wolf passed the lead wolf — a female, lighter and faster. She reached Tek's flank, snapping at him to edge him off the path and into the brush, where it would be easier for her to pounce on him.

Tek knew that if this wolf got him off the path she would kill him, and then follow the other wolves down the path to their main prey — the cub. Later they would come back to include his meager flesh in their day's meal.

With a desperate burst of speed Tek edged ahead of the wolf's snapping jaws. It was a short burst, but it got him to a place on the path where a heavy swath of pine needles saved him. In the slip–sliding needles, Tek's claws had the advantage over the wolves' blunter toenails. The wolves lost more speed than Tek did as they all dug for grip.

Dashing out into a clearing that sloped down to a stream, Tek glimpsed the dark brown mass of the mother bear's back moving slowly through the grass, about halfway down the slope.

Now that he was close enough to the mother bear to be heard, Tek squalled out a warning with as much breath as he could spare — which was very little, for the wolves were catching up again.

But the bear heard the odd noise and whirled around. Rearing up on her hind legs, she saw the wolves coming fast, close behind the blur of skinny lynx. She growled a quick warning to her cub and roared out a fierce challenge to the wolves.

She was a terrifying sight, with every fiber of her massive body readied to protect her cub. But the wolves only quickened their rush on her. They had lost the advantage of surprise because of the scrawny, strange–smelling lynx, but they still had the crucial edge. There were no trees nearby, for the cub to climb to safety. They would surround the mother and bait, harry and distract her, staying just out of her reach, until the crucial moment when one of them would slip in and snatch the cub away.

Tek raced past the bear and took up a position next to her cub, which was confused and frightened. If it panicked it might bolt away from its mother's shelter. Tek chuffed at it reassuringly, to steady it.

In moments the clearing reverberated with the roars and growls of the bear, and the snarls and snapping jaws of the wolves.

The four wolves worked in two pairs. The lead male and the lighter faster female faced the bear, making rapid, coordinated feints and sharp nips at her, while the other two wolves made well–timed dives at her flanks, and her cub. They forced her to twist constantly, rapidly to cover her cub.

The wolves' movements had the confidence and lethal efficiency of long experience hunting together, but the bear was not bereft of experience in fighting off wolves. She stayed on her hind legs as much as possible, keeping her head high, out of their reach. This signaled to the wolves that she had some experience, but she also deceived them. She limited the range and speed of her paws as they swiped through the air to bat at the wolves, causing the wolves think that she was a much older and weaker bear than she actually was. Emboldened, they jumped in closer, getting in some hard tearing bites at her instead of nips. Several times she let them bite her, until they were overconfident. And in really close. In a sudden rush she lunged at the lead wolf and killed him in an instant, snapping his neck with the full strength and reach of her paw.

Even before his body flew limply away from the impact, the bear rushed the female wolf at her front, raking her neck with her claws before she could twist herself beyond reach.

The bear had attacked the male first, even though it was the female that had been nipping and biting at her the most. Now maddened by the fight, the bear blazed to pursue the wounded female as she fell away from her, snarling a challenge. But her cub's cry and Tek's sharp yowl behind her quickly brought her to her senses. She whirled in time to swipe rapidly and violently at the two flanking wolves as they closed in on her cub.

While those two wolves backed off slightly and joined with the wounded female to regroup, the bear suddenly seized her cub by its scruff and raced toward the trees along the stream. Tek hurried after them. Possibly the wolves would not pursue them, with one fewer in their number and another wounded. And if the bear could reach the trees ahead of the wolves, her cub would be able to climb one to safety.

But the wolves did pursue, and caught up with the bear well before she reached the trees. They closed on her again, forcing her to drop her cub and whirl to fight them.

This time the wolves were more wary, but they still expected to get the cub away from its mother in the end. It would just take longer to wear her down, until she made a mistake that would be fatal for her cub.

The three wolves spaced themselves out in a rough circle around the bear, worrying at her front and sides, while Tek fought them with tooth and claw when they got too close to her cub at her back.

The cub was squalling. Up until then it had borne up well enough, but shock, fear and confusion were addling it. Its mother grunted at it, to steady it. Tek called to it and, while keeping the wolves as much at bay as he could, he batted the cub in the direction of the trees by the stream.

Both the cub and its mother began to respond to Tek's efforts to guide the cub. Given a part to perform in the fight, the cub lost some of its fear. And its mother, despite the distractions of fighting the three wolves, understood that the lynx was trying to move the fight closer to the trees. Now as she fought she edged herself backward in that direction.

But the wolves adapted quickly. The wounded wolf, which was now the leader, shifted around the bear to place itself and another of the wolves between the bear and the stream, making it much more difficult for her to reach her goal.

The battle raged on, each side losing some power and speed, but gaining a better understanding of the other side's strengths and weaknesses. The new lead wolf was aggressive and the most skillful fighter of the wolves. It set the pace, forcing the bear to react defensively. The wolves were still working to wear the bear down, and enrage her into making the mistake of lunging at the lead wolf — just far enough away from her cub for one of the two other wolves to rush in and snatch it.

The strange lynx at the cub's side was an unexpected complication, but it was obviously tiring and they did not expect it to last much longer.

Ever since the cub had settled down enough to keep itself safer in the battle, Tek had been saving some of his remaining strength for a bold move.

Working to break down the bear's endurance, the wolves had settled into a rhythm of advances and retreats. They used different patterns, but their patterns became predictable. Tek chose the moment when the lead wolf began yet another lunge toward the bear's left, while the other wolf at the bear's front started its whip around to harry the bear's right flank. Tek gave his most powerful snarl to signal to the bear that he was charging, and he rushed out from between her legs, attacking the lead wolf as she advanced. He got his teeth into the wolf's neck wounds, and jerked and tore at them madly.

After an instant of surprise the second frontal wolf whipped back to savage the lynx dangling from the lead wolf's neck. Both wolves were backing away from the bear, but not quickly enough. The bear saw in these moments of imbalance the opportunity to bring her great head down at last. She dropped and pivoted, charging the third wolf behind her in a rush of flashing teeth. She was so amazingly fast on all fours that she got one of its forelegs between her teeth and nearly bitten off before the wolf could jerk its leg free and tumble away yelping.

The bear had already swung back around to the other two wolves, so fast that they had not gotten very far back from her, and the second frontal wolf had not yet reached Tek. The bear charged the second wolf, clamping her teeth on its neck and jerking it off its feet, whipping it about while beating and mauling its flanks with her claws.

Even with Tek hanging on to the lead wolf's neck she charged the bear's head and got her teeth into the side of the bear's neck. But she could not get a deep hold through the bear's thick fur and neck folds.

The bear made a grunting noise that Tek recognized: it was a sound she had often made in the den, when signaling her feeding cub or Tek to release her nipple. Tek understood and immediately released his hold on the lead wolf's neck, falling and scrambling away to take up his position beside the cub.

The bear shook off the lead wolf and knocked it nearly senseless with a powerful swipe of paw. Dazed, the lead wolf could not help the wolf whose neck was still in the bear's jaws. Its struggles ended quickly: the bear chomped down on its neck and it no longer moved of its own accord.

The two remaining wolves — the wounded lead wolf and the one with the maimed leg — retreated and watched from a distance as the bear and the lynx ate the most recently killed wolf. They silently left the clearing long before the bear and lynx finished with that one, and proceeded with the cub to the other one, where they ate their fill of it as well.

The cub sniffed at the blood of the dead wolves and licked it curiously, but it was going to be a while before it could eat flesh. When the cub bawled and nuzzled its mother for some milk she sat back from her kill, and let it nurse.

*   *   *

In the clearing — which had regained its ordinary quiet — the bear sat in the sun, a colossal mound with one of her bloody paws draped over her nursing cub, looking on as the small lynx tore and worried at wolf sinew and bones for bits of flesh.

She was not sure what she was going to do about this creature, which was by far the oddest she had ever encountered.

It had the shape and scent of lynx, but it also smelled of the two-legged ones that sometimes hunted her kind in the lands lower down, along the great waterways that some of the mountain streams ran to. It was odd for a lynx to have this second scent. But oddest of all was the scent that had overlaid the other two: it was one that she associated with her own essence, of bear.

That scent on the lynx had seemed to require something of her. That was why she had not killed it, when she unexpectedly found it in her den. That was why she had tolerated its inexplicable presence there since then, and allowed it to nurse after one of her two cubs had died.

Gradually though, in the months since she had given birth, the essence of bear faded away from this strange interloper, until it was entirely gone when she awoke this morning. So she did not let it nurse, and she had intended to chase it away when she returned to her den, if it was still there. She did not feel any obligation to it; it no longer belonged with her.

But now . . .

The great she–bear was capable of understanding that the lynx, grateful to her, had warned her of the wolves' approach. But she could not have expected anything else that it had done.

It had steadied her panicky cub and kept the wolves away from it, when the fight was at its most desperate for her. And it had tried to help her get her cub to the safety of a tree.

But strangest of all — and incomprehensible — was the lynx's sudden attack on the wolves. No normal lynx would ever do that.

15

The wolf it attacked nearly got it in its teeth, just before it twisted itself past the wolf's jaws, and latched onto the wolf's wounded neck. The lynx would have died if the wolf had gotten its teeth into it. And for what? The lynx was not the cub's mother; it was not even a female. Perhaps . . . the bear's floating thoughts turned to the odd scent of the two–leggers that was part of this lynx.

The bear did not have a pack–hunting mentality. She understood that there was a loyalty among pack members such as wolves and two–leggers, but she could not connect that knowledge with what the lynx had done. She could not understand that when the lynx attacked the wolf it had relied on her to use the opportunity it had created, for her to take down another one of the wolves, and to save the lynx if possible, while she did so. She *had* used that opportunity, but *not* as a member of a two–member pack with the lynx. She used it instead as a bear would use any advantage that came its way in a fight. And the lynx seemed to understand that about her. Her thoughts looped around again to that two–legger scent in this lynx.

* * *

Tek noticed that the bear was watching him. Unsure of what the bear's disposition would be, he turned to face it, as the cub finished suckling.

The cub scampered over to Tek. Naturally rambunctious, this male cub had a full measure of confidence, buoyancy, and aggression. He felt safe again and satiated, and he reveled in the sunshine that seemed to melt through his deep brown fur and into his bones. Living fully in the moment, he wanted nothing more than to spar and play with his brother in this glorious, sumptuous place. He rushed his skinny brother, bowled him over and chewed on his ear until his brother squirmed away from his grip and batted him away.

The mother bear got up and led the way down to the stream. There she and Tek drank, letting the cold water flow over their wounds. The mother bear had the most wounds and the deepest, having taken the brunt of the fight.

When the mother bear and cub returned up the long slope to the den in the forest, Tek followed but did not go inside the den. Instead, he found an old burrow nearby that he enlarged until he could fit himself inside to sleep in it. The next morning when the mother bear let her cub out of their den, the cub quickly sniffed out the burrow, and pestered his scrawny brother until he crawled out and joined them.

Over the next two moons the odd threesome often ranged and foraged together. The mother bear usually tolerated Tek's presence, but as her cub grew it changed toward Tek. It came to realize that Tek was not actually its brother.

On the edges of the mother bear's territory, the mother and cub occasionally met other mother bears with their cubs. One of them was a daughter of the cub's mother, which was not unusual because mothers often permitted their daughters to have territories next to their own. As the cub rolled and sparred with the other cubs, including some that were closely related to him, he began to understand that his own brother was very different from them. It did not resemble the other cubs at all, and its scent was nothing like theirs.

Then came the day when the cub caught the fresh scent of a lynx that had crossed over the path leading down to the stream. It was a simpler scent than his brother's . . . in this simpler form it was starkly different from everything that the cub knew of as bear.

The cub's mother was close behind it on the path. When she reached the scent she grunted to her cub to be on watch and wary. A lynx rarely bothered a bear cub, unless the cub was orphaned or badly hurt. But she was warning her cub that this scent was from a creature that was an enemy of bears, though it was not as fearsome as wolves.

The mother bear continued down the path but the cub remained, waiting for its brother to reach the spot.

Tek had been delayed. He had gone off the path to catch a mouse. Mice were hardly ever worth the effort they cost him, but at least there was the satisfaction of reducing it from an elusive blur, to a limp morsel between his teeth.

When Tek reached where the cub was waiting for him on the path, he too scented the drifting odor of lynx. He put his kill down and circled. Female lynx, cutting across the bear path, going easterly down the mountain. Probably heading for the boggy area, where turkey and grouse often fed on the striped snakes that were plentiful there.

The cub seized the dead mouse and chewed on it. With a new look in its eyes, the cub watched Tek approach to get his mouse back. The new look lacked the old acceptance, and it bordered on an aggressive rejection. Tek stopped. He understood that he should not get too close to the cub, or ever expect friendliness from it again.

From further down the path came the chuff of the mother bear, calling to her cub to catch up with her. The cub left, taking Tek's mouse with it.

Tek went his own way that day, following neither the familiar scent of the bears nor the new scent of the lynx. On his own in the forest, for the first time in a long time, he tried again to shape shift from lynx into boy. But still, he could not do it.

He ranged farther than ever from the bears' den, though he still kept high up on the mountain. If there were any of the People living below the mountain, by the rivers or the broader streams, Tek still wanted to be able to approach them as a boy, if he approached them at all.

As he searched for a new place to sleep that night, a loneliness stole over him. A normal lynx would prefer to be alone almost of the time, but he was not a normal lynx. He was of the People; as such he had their need to be part of a group that watched over and helped each other, and sometimes fought with each other, in the struggle to survive.

The cub had been attached to Tek as long as it thought that Tek was its brother. Knowing better than that all along, Tek had cared for the cub like a true brother, and still did. He missed the acceptance that the cub — until that day — had given him. He also missed being within the protection of the cub's powerful mother. She had tolerated him, and in return he had helped her with her cub as much as he could.

But all of that was over now. He was on his own. Life was going to be lonelier for him, and a lot more dangerous.

Eventually he found an abandoned burrow and settled into it for the night. None too soon: heavy splats of rain fell soon after he had curled up inside it. A heavy, late summer storm rolled in, with sky–splitting lightning, and thunder that shook the mountain to its core.

Safe in his dry burrow, Tek's thoughts ranged over the stories he had heard as a child, of the thunder birds — the giant black spirit birds swooping low over the mountains in their fierce mock battles. They made lightning with the clack and clash of their long beaks, and thunder with the rake of their huge wings, as they spun away and then back toward each other in battling rounds. Tek kept his eyes closed until the flashing and rumbling receded, for it was said to be dangerous to meet the red–eyed gaze of the great birds during a storm. When at length the rain softened, it lulled him to sleep, and then into a strange dream.

He dreamed that after the storm a huge bear shoved its snout into his burrow, snorting insistently for him to come out. With dream–washed surprise Tek obeyed the bear immediately, because he recognized it: it was the great, scentless spirit bear that he had met once before, on the night he and the other shapeshifters pursued Okat in her panther form, when she disrupted the parting ceremony after her mother's death.

As Tek scrambled out of the burrow, in his dream he shapeshifted effortlessly into a boy — except that he was a boy no longer. He was the size of a full–grown man! He could not see much of himself in the darkness, but he could feel that his chest was broader and his limbs were longer. He was definitely bigger all over, with a man's strength. But he could also feel that his body was covered with scars that went deep into his flesh, from the many wounds he had sustained in the final, desperate fight with Okat.

The bear signaled for Tek to follow it. He kept up with it easily at first. It was always a large darker shape out ahead of him, unmistakably different from everything else.

The bear led Tek further up the mountain, where the way became so steep that Tek had to climb on all fours. In his dream he felt as if he climbed a very long time, until at last some diffused light came into his surroundings, like the light of dawn. But he could not see much of his surroundings, because by then he was climbing in a mist with only the bear's shadowy mass ahead of him.

19

The land under him leveled off, so that he could again walk upright. Then as the mist cleared the spirit bear ahead of him disappeared, and he found himself alone in a vast forested plateau.

This forest was very beautiful, and a hunter's paradise. With his heightened ability to scent, Tek knew that the forest was chock full of all kinds of animals, and was especially plentiful with deer, wolves, grouse and turkey.

He continued on in the same direction that the spirit bear had been leading him.

Along his way he passed by a thin but excellent vein of flint in an outcropping of rock. All around the rock there was knap litter on the ground. He found a likely striker and stooped to knap off a few pieces of flint for himself. Although he was deep in a dream, to do this made perfect sense to him: good flint was hard to find, and made the best weapons and tools. He struck off several small pieces and took the best two. But because he had neither clothes nor a pouch, he carried them in his mouth, wedged along either side of his lower jaw.

Soon afterward Tek came to a clearing. Approaching it quietly, he observed that there was a bark shelter in the center, similar to the type that the People built when they were hunting far from their knat. But by the side of this shelter there was something unusual: thick saplings had been cut and lashed together to form a sturdy cage, and inside the cage was a young bear — no longer a cub, but not yet its full size.

The bear started squalling. It sounded to Tek as if it was hungry.

An old woman came out of the shelter with a long stick. She viciously jabbed and hit at the cub through the sapling bars of the cage until the bear quieted.

In the distance behind Tek he heard someone approaching. He hid, and watched as two hunters arrived at the clearing, carrying their kill — a very large deer — lashed to a carrying pole.

A segment of time dissolved in the dream, until it was night, and the smell of roasted deer meat permeated the clearing. Tek was still hiding in the bushes when the old woman came out of the shelter, carrying some cleanly stripped bones. She shoved them through the top of the bear's cage. The bear cried, as if pleading for food.

Apparently, it was not being given any of the meat; only bare bones to gnaw on.

In his dream, Tek resolved to free the bear that night. He thought that might be why the great, scentless bear had led him here — to free the caged bear. But he had his own reasons as well. The bear in the cage reminded him of the cub that he still thought of as a little brother. It also bothered him that the old woman was so cruel to the bear. Why, he asked himself, in the midst of all the plentiful game in this forest, did she keep this wild creature captive, beating it when it cried, and giving it only stripped bones to eat?

When the night was very still Tek shapeshifted to lynx and crept into the clearing. Upon reaching the bear's cage he shapeshifted back into a man — for in his dream he was still a man rather than a boy.

Oddly, as he approached the cage it seemed to get bigger, or perhaps it was that he got smaller. By the time he reached it, both it and the bear inside it seemed to tower over him. He had to climb up the side of the cage, in order to reach the top.

There he worked with the larger of his two pieces of flint, cutting at the lashing that held three of the saplings in place across the top of the cage. When he was done, the bear would be able to climb out through the gap.

Inside the cage the bear watched him in silence. It looked emaciated — hardly more than skin and bones. Tek also noticed that there was a length of cord around its neck, with a short, frayed piece of the cord trailing from the knot, as if the cord had once been longer but had broken or worn away.

The moment Tek got the third sapling cut loose he jumped down from the cage and backed away from it, beckoning for the bear to come out. The further he got from the cage, the more he returned to his normal size.

At first the bear did not move. Thinking that the bear was afraid of him in his full–size man form, Tek shapeshifted into a buck. There could be no reason for a young, weakened bear to fear a deer buck.

All had been very quiet in the clearing, but while Tek was shapeshifting to buck he reflexively glanced around. Shock jolted through him when he saw the old woman standing in the shelter's doorway, watching him!

At that moment the bear scrambled out of the cage and ran from the clearing as fast as it could. For an emaciated bear that had been cage–bound it moved very fast, though awkwardly, with heavy grunts of effort. Tek bounded away after it. But behind them the woman shouted rolling words he did not understand, and within moments he was falling through a dark sky. He fell upside down with his buck legs flailing above him — faster and faster he fell until his back collided with something large and dark that gave a little under him — something that smelled of feathers.

Then he was slipping off the large black wing feathers of a huge shadowy bird, and down onto the wing feathers of another huge bird that was wheeling just below it. Soon he was slipping off that dark wing as well, but the bird from above had swung around below to catch him again on one of its wings. As each bird swooped and wheeled, lightning flashed as their beaks clashed, and thunder crashed and rolled off their wings.

Each drop from wing to wing, seemed to slightly slow down time. There was a slight bounce as the stiff wing feathers gave a little under his falling weight, and the slide of his fur across the jagged peaks and valleys formed by the shafts and vanes of the birds' enormous flight feathers.

Tek continued downward, with the two birds slowing his fall, until he was not far above a large lake. He slipped off a wing for the last time and fell until he splashed down into the lake's bitterly cold water.

In the last dream fragments Tek bobbed up and swam for the lake shore. It was a long way to swim. When he reached the shore he collapsed there as a buck.

Chapter 3

It was morning when Tek awoke as a lynx in a snow burrow, nestled in a thick layer of leaves that were covered over with snow. He poked his head out. Most of the trees were bare, though oaks and beeches had clinging brown leaves.

It was a bright, clear day. He sensed, from the lightness of the air and the sweep of its currents, that he was on high land, probably in high hills or low mountains. Much of the land was white with snow, but a few patches of leaf litter mottled the ground. It was definitely winter here but the air was not frigid. From the look of things, some past snowfalls had packed down, and a thaw of several days was not quite over.

Time seemed to have moved strangely, because when he had last gone to sleep it had been late summer.

All of the scents had subtly changed again. They were not the same as when he had lived among the People; nor were they the same as the more recent time when he had lived with the mother bear and her cub. It was as if everything had shifted slightly away from what it had been before.

He felt very much older. At first he thought his limbs were just stiff from the cold and dampness, but when he had warmed up by moving about, his joints still felt loose and sore, as if altered for the worse by age.

There was a lake nearby, so he went to its shore to drink. On his way, after checking the scents around him for danger, he felt safe enough to shapeshift into a boy. But he found that he could not do it. In his strange, vivid dream last night, he had shapeshifted so easily into a man and then a buck. Now he was stuck in his lynx form.

As he lapped up water he felt something hard and sharp wedged between his lower jaw and cheek. He worked it loose with his tongue, spat it onto his paw.

It was a small piece of flint.

It was one of the two pieces that he had struck and put inside his mouth to take with him on his journey, in his dream. The other one he had lost after using it to free the emaciated bear from its cage.

That had been a dream. And yet, here was one of the pieces of flint from his dream, exactly as he remembered it . . .

He slipped the piece of flint back into its niche inside his mouth and hunkered down beside the lake shore to think. He labored to make sense of all that had happened to him between when he had first been able to shapeshift into a lynx — right before the brutal battle with Okat — and this moment.

When he was done thinking about it, he was no longer certain whether he was fully alive, or had died to some extent — perhaps fully — in the battle with Okat.

Because of the strangeness of the scents around him, and the aged aching in his bones, he no longer knew whether he was in the time that he had been born into, or in some later time.

And because of the piece of flint, he was not sure how much of his dream had actually been real.

Tek rested beside the lake until the sun was nearly midway across the sky. The sunlight on his dark mottled fur sank into his body, soothing his aching sinews and bones. At length he decided to find a place where the water ran out from the lake. If he was, as he thought, in some hills or mountains, he would follow the water down the slopes until he reached a river. There he hoped to find a knat of the People, where he could observe them from a safe distance, and perhaps get in close enough to listen to their talk.

Tek padded along the edge of the lake until he found a brook flowing from it, which he followed down slope. Due to the thaw, much of the snow alongside the brook had receded, making it easier for him to travel beside it. For the rest of that day and the next three days, he went generally downward through forested slopes alongside ever–widening watercourses, through marshy thickets and an occasional forest clearing. As he descended the amount of snow on the ground lessened, but most of the time it was still easiest to travel close to the waterways.

Whenever the waterways split, he followed the wider course, until he was going along a waterway that became very wide and ran turbulently through a broad clearing, surrounded by forested hills. There Tek caught a hare. Its flesh was sour and tough but by then he was ravenous.

It was while he was eating the hare that he thought the shape of the hills in the distance looked familiar — they were something like the hills that rose above the knat of his birth.

It was exciting to think that he might be getting close to a knat of the People, but he also intended to be cautious. When darkness came, he continued downward out of the hills because, if he *was* getting anywhere close to a knat, he preferred to reach it while it was still dark. In his lynx form, he would be able to observe the knat much more easily under cover of darkness, than during the day.

During his journey there had been much less scent of forest creatures than he had expected there to be. And the scent of everything still differed from what he had been used to.

Near the middle of the night he reached a place where the waterway split again. This time he followed the narrower course, which was a creek that had cut down through slabs of shale, with hemlocks covering the slopes on both sides. He followed the creek because it felt vaguely familiar, though he still recognized nothing — neither the terrain nor the scents.

He was going along a deer trail on a ridge that rose gradually from the creek bed, when he caught faint wafts of wood smoke in the air, and something like the scent of the People. But there were new scents mixed in – strange animal scents that Tek did not recognize.

The scent of the wood smoke triggered a great longing in Tek, to shapeshift back into a boy, if only for a little while. But when he tried to, he could not do it.

About then he found that he was exceptionally weary, so he decided to wait a day before getting any closer to the scents that both enticed him, and repelled him. He made his way down to the creek where he drank and, after crossing the creek and angling up away

25

from it, he found an abandoned burrow, which still smelled faintly of hare. The burrow was close to the base of a tree, and opened up enough behind a large overhanging tree root for him to squirm into it. It was cramped, but it was dry and would do for a few hours of sleep.

He slept through to morning.

He was still peacefully asleep when something poked into his ribs. Instantly awake, he found that a stick with two blunt points had been thrust into the burrow. He let out a yowl of pain and surprise as the stick was quickly twisted into the folds of his fur, and then tugged.

If he had been a hare, he would have been yanked right out of the hole by the stick's prongs, which were wound tight into the skin under his fur. But as a lynx in a burrow that was too small for him, the tugged stick simply jammed him against the burrow wall. Growling, he pushed himself back enough to grab the stick with his teeth and worry it, trying to free his fur from the stick's points.

* * *

Outside of the burrow, the old woman who wielded the stick was at least as surprised as Tek was — but not because the animal in the burrow was not a hare. Her surprise was because the animal — a lynx or bobcat by the sound of it — had seized her stick and would not let it go. In all of the many years that she had hunted hare like this, by poking a forked stick into their burrows and then twisting it, the cornered animal had never, ever fought back. She was instantly concerned that it might have the madness that sometimes beset the forest creatures, causing their mouths to drip with a foamy saliva, and causing them to attack irrationally. She let go of her stick and stepped well back from the burrow, with her club held in both hands, ready to clout the animal if it rushed at her.

The woman's name was Phoebe Carr. She lived nearby, alone. She was very old, unsteady from hunger and an ailing heart, and her vision was not as good as it had once been. Her thin hands flexed on her club, as she continued to back further away from the burrow.

The stick waggled on the ground in front of the burrow. It seemed to Phoebe that it was turning, opposite to the way she had twisted it.

26

When the stick stopped moving, a gaunt old lynx slunk out of the hole. Phoebe had never seen a lynx — or any other animal for that matter — as battle-scarred as this one: all of its fur was disfigured by scars that crisscrossed its body, and there were many jagged punctures that had healed over unevenly.

The lynx stood in front of the burrow, staring back at her balefully. Phoebe could not see any foaming saliva around its mouth, but she was still wary. A normal lynx would have dashed away. This one stared back at her more like a wolf would, or a coyote — or even . . . a person. Her imagination stirred, and she thought that this lynx had a look in its eyes that was almost human. Her thoughts tumbled around uneasily, disjointedly culling through tales half-remembered from her childhood, of witches' familiars, and demon changelings.

*   *   *

Tek had no fear of the strange woman. She was obviously quite old, weak and alone. He took his time, absorbing her strangeness. She wore long-skirted clothing that was not made of hide; it smelt of animal hair and plant, under a wood smoke smell. The skin of her face and hands was unusually pale, and her eyes were not dark like eyes were supposed to be — they were a light grey color. The structure of her face was also different from anything he had ever seen before. With a face like that she could not possibly be one of the People. And yet she was similar to them, in the way that a crested grouse was similar to a spruce grouse. He struggled for a term to associate with the woman's scent, and the other scents she carried with her that were strange to him. He settled upon thinking of her as an Other.

*   *   *

Phoebe broke the standoff by taking a deliberate step backward, away from the lynx. Perceiving this, the lynx tilted its head quizzically, and then took a deliberate step away from her and away from the burrow. Then for every step backward that Phoebe made, the lynx made one as well. But by its manner the lynx made it clear that it was not retreating: it moved with a fearlessness, almost an impudence, as if it was mocking her by copying her movements. This spooked Phoebe further.

The two of them continued to step further away from each other, until at length the lynx lost interest in the proceedings. It turned and simply disappeared behind some bushes growing near the side of the creek.

But just before the lynx left, it uttered a low chuffing noise, as if it was admonishing Phoebe for having poked at it.

* * *

Phoebe stood watching and listening for a while, and then picked up her stick and cautiously made her way home.

She was disappointed that she would go meatless again today, but her mind was busy thinking about this odd lynx, and what she could do to protect herself, if it hung around here and proved to be dangerous.

Her heart thudded dully in her chest — no actual pain this time, but in the past month or so it had stuttered from time to time, as it did now. She knew that the pains and odd thumpings probably meant that her heart was going to give out before long. And there had been death omens —six crows in her dooryard one morning . . . a dark grey shape in mist by the creek. Death was coming, and would soon reach her.

She accepted this, and had only one simple wish — to die quietly in her sleep, in her home, when a natural death could no longer be forestalled. She certainly did *not* want death to come out in the open, from the attack of a wild animal.

For a long while she had been the oldest person in the valley, a full generation older than everyone else. Nearly half a century ago she had come from an eastern coastal town with her husband and some other relatives. They were all so young and hopeful then, seeking land of their own for farming. Eagerly they had gone west, sometimes on the great east–west river, other times along the raw corduroy roads through wilderness. It was still called the Dark Country, because whenever the road veered away from the settlements along the river, it went on for miles and miles through a shadowy darkness under the boughs of ancient trees.

Eventually Phoebe's family and another related family found land they could afford here, in a forested valley, across the wide river from a small settlement, while the others who were with them chose to continue west in their search for land. Later, an unrelated family also settled in the valley. All three families carved homesteads out of the forest, toiling through the youth and prime of their lives to clear fields, build homes and barns, and rear their children. They eked sustenance from the land while the forest loomed close by. And all throughout little valleys like this one, on both sides of the river, others were doing much the same.

The endeavors of some families succeeded well enough, but the fortunes of others — including Phoebe's — waned. Her immediate family died off from illness, accidents, or death in the earlier of two indian raids that had come five years apart. For many years now she had been the only one of her own family that was left, living out her years on her homestead, most of it long since overgrown. The cabin and barn had gone up in flames during the raids; she lived on in a hut that had once been one of the farm's outbuildings. A stone hearth and chimney had been built onto one end of it for her cooking and heat, and a sturdy shed had been added onto the back to house a cow. The homestead's fields had gone to brush and small trees, except for one small field that was worked to provide enough hay for her cow, and a little extra for barter.

Phoebe was distantly related to the large and growing Tutner family that had their homestead about two miles away from hers — it was by far the largest homestead of the three in the valley. Years ago, the Tutners had suggested that Phoebe come and live with them — and work for her keep, of course. But she had refused their offer. She knew she would be treated as a servant, even though she was related to them, and it was well known that the Tutners worked all of their servants and slaves uncommonly hard. So she remained apart, and independent, even though, of late, that meant she went hungry more often than not.

* * *

Over the next several weeks Phoebe never saw the lynx. But she knew it was in the area, and was actually skulking around her home. After each new snow she found fresh lynx prints, often around the outside of the cow shed that shared the back wall of her home.

* * *

Tek had easily followed the woman's scent back to where she lived. Her home was by itself in the woods, not far from the creek. Like the woman, her home was unlike anything he had ever seen before. It was small like a hunting camp, but it was not made of lashed saplings and layers of bark. Instead, stacks of logs were joined at the corners and smeared over with mud. Above the logs rose a sharply angled roof, covered with rows of a small, flat pieces of wood. And instead of having a proper smoke hole, the smoke came out of a tower of flat stones, also smeared over with mud, that were stacked up on one end of the structure.

There were two openings in the walls of the structure for the woman to go in and out — one in front and the other in the back, but these openings were not covered with hides or woven mats. Instead, solid, flat pieces of wood filled the openings and made a weird creaking noise as they were pulled or pushed sideways to open and close. There was a small vent opening on all four sides of the structure, high up, that had wood covers on their inner sides. The one in front also had a hard, clear surface on its outer side.

But what completely mystified Tek was the large creature that lived in the structure with the woman — at least, it was always inside at night. During the day when the weather was sunny the creature was let out to move about in a small fenced area at the back of the structure.

Tek was first attracted to the back of the structure because of the plentiful scent of mouse and rat there. Late one night he squeezed inside, past a damaged piece of the flat wood that covered the entrance. Inside he found that there was a stout wall between this part of the structure, where the large creature was housed, and the rest of it, where the woman lived. There was an opening in the wall in between, but it was firmly blocked by another one of those flat wooden barriers — one that had no damaged places in it for him to squeeze through.

The large creature stirred while Tek explored its living space, but it did not seem overly concerned by his presence. Its body was nearly as big around as a moose, but its four legs were much shorter and heavier. The head and neck seemed too big for the rest of the body, and it had a long, thin tail that it tossed around its other end.

Strangest of all, it had a large hairless pouch between its back legs with several big teats on it, often swollen and dripping with mother's milk. The milk pouch puzzled Tek, not only because of its size and strange shape, but also because the creature had no young with it, to drink the milk.

Tek did not know what to call the creature; he eventually settled on thinking of it as a bess, because that was the word that the woman used when she called to it.

In this part of the structure, some hides had been lashed to the wooden framing overhead, and the hides held some mounds of dry, sweet–smelling grasses. Some rodent scent wafted down from this loft, but most of the scent was concentrated in the straw strewn over the dirt floor. It was especially strong where the straw had built up in the corners.

The rodents retreated into their holes whenever Tek entered the structure. He settled himself in the shadows near where the draft left the structure, and waited for them to come back out, once they were emboldened by his stillness. He usually forewent the small mice that were the first to venture out; his patience was rewarded by a larger one, or by a water rat.

When he was done eating, he disposed of the scant remains in the forest, away from the woman's home. And when he returned to the structure, he carefully set his paws in his prior tracks through the snow. For he had already decided that he was going to live secretly in her home, at least until the Snow Moon's time[5] was over. The fewer tracks he made, the less apparent his presence would be.

For a moon or so he had a life of relative ease. Rodent prey was fairly plentiful, and he had a warm, comfortable place to sleep and rest during the day. But he did not regain all of his former strength; he did not come to feel young and strong again, as he thought he should. He winded quickly; he tired easily. And try as he might he could not shape shift back into a boy. But there was nothing he could do about it except yield to caution, compensating for the limits of his strength and speed.

---

[5] February, usually

He made himself more and more at home around the old woman's place, sleeping off and on throughout the day in the loft above the bess, burrowed in the dry grasses. It was up there that he discovered a small gap in the flat pieces of wood that separated the bess's living space from the rest of the structure. Through that gap he observed the old woman as she moved about in her part of the inside space.

When she was up and about she moved very slowly, with little change in her daily routine. At the beginning of each day, she tended to the bess, and that was how Tek learned that the creature actually allowed the old woman to take its milk — for herself! When she squeezed the bess's teats the milk hissed into a bowl, and the woman drank the milk or mixed it with her food.

Tek was deeply shocked the first time he saw the woman drinking the bess's milk. It was so unnatural to keep an animal for its milk. The People would never do that. And yet, the bess and the woman acted as if it was perfectly normal.

Everything else the woman did seemed fairly ordinary. Mostly she stayed inside, keeping a small fire going only on coldest days. She sat for hours on end doing some kind of work with a fluffy hair that smelled of animal, using the light from the high openings, mainly the one with the clear surface. First she smoothed the fluff and then she twisted it into long strands that she wound onto sticks. When she went out it was usually to haul in some snow or some creek water for her cooking and for drinking.

Tek was fascinated by the woman's tools, a few of which were in the bess's space. They were made of wood and an odd, cold substance that was hard like flint, but not as brittle. The cold substance was wonderfully shaped for the purpose of the tool, and made the tools very strong. They did not break very easily, or go dull as quickly as bone, or chip as easily as flint.

Most of the time the woman was silent, except that she sometimes talked to the bess, and every night she spoke some words before going to sleep. Tek did not know the meaning of her words, or why she lived alone. She did not seem unhappy to be alone, but there was no one to go out hunting for her, and she did not have much to eat. Sometimes she sighed and rubbed her stomach or laid down during the day, like he had seen his own People do — like he himself had done — when there was hunger and nothing to eat.

She was old and weak, and sometimes she stopped what she was doing and hunched over, pressing her hands against her chest, rocking herself with labored breathing. Tek had seen that too, among the older ones of his own People, when their hearts were paining them.

When the weather was too cold or the snow too deep, Tek stayed inside at night, and was sometimes able to catch one of the dwindling number of rats and mice. But most nights he went out, hunting and exploring the countryside.

He quickly discovered that the old woman's home was in a little valley, surrounded by heavily forested hills, except on one side where a good–sized river ran through the area. Much of the valley floor was forested but there were two other cleared areas, where Others lived. Both of those areas were larger than the old woman's place; one of them was much larger. They both had the scents of Others of varying ages — especially the larger of the two. Many strange scents wafted from both of these cleared areas, that Tek could not identify — scents of unfamiliar foods, animals, birds and goods, in concentrations suggestive of plenty, relative to the amount of cleared space. Tek wondered all the more about why his Other — the old woman — lived alone and in want as she did. He thought it was a very unnatural way for anyone to live, especially a woman.

The old woman's place, besides being the smallest cleared area by far, was also the one furthest back from the river. The largest of the three was closest to the river, and next to a stream that emptied into it. The other was also near the river, but farther back and on the other side of the stream.

The river was broad. It was not iced over, and Tek judged that it was probably too wide and swift for him to easily swim across it. But he was not really interested in crossing it, at least not while it was still winter. Only the scents of more Others and more forest wafted over from across the river. He could not detect any of the scents that he associated with his own People.

The old woman's place only had the small structure where she lived with the bess. But the other two clearings both had more and larger structures. Most of the structures were clustered together something like a knat, but they were not surrounded by a protective wall of spiked logs, like a knat would be.

Tek was very curious about these Others and their structures, and their unfamiliar scents. But he could only observe them from a distance, because of the wolf–like creatures that lived with them, and bellowed a fierce cacophony of howls and yelps the moment they sensed that he — or any other night creature — was anywhere near. Even when he kept downwind of them, they were quick to make their raucous, threatening commotion the moment they heard the sound of his careful, nearly silent footfalls. Tek named them howlers, for the awful outcry they made.

Normally when he crept too close to where they lived, the howlers did not chase him — he later found out that they were usually tied up or shut in an enclosure at night. One did chase him into the forest one night, but he was able to keep well ahead of it. By then he knew the forest around there rather well, and it was one of the older howlers that was chasing him — he could tell by its more faded howls and by how quickly he was able to outdistance it. It also seemed to Tek that this howler was not so bold when it was out in the forest alone, separated from the rest of the howlers.

It was a few nights afterward that Tek realized how fortunate he had been, to have been chased by only one of the older howlers, with no Others in on the chase. That was also the night Tek discovered that these Others had a magic long stick that made thunder and lightning — a stick that could kill whatever it was pointed at!

There had been a bear in the area — the smaller type that was black rather than brown. Tek had scented it in the vicinity of the two Other clearings so often that he suspected it was attracted to where the Others lived, perhaps by something it wanted to eat. Whenever the howlers scented the bear, they went nearly berserk, with a special frenzy to their noise.

On that night Tek was not too far from the old woman's home when he heard howlers' noise start up in the distance, from where the larger of the two clusters of Others was. By the sound of it, he knew the howlers had scented the bear. But instead of the noise staying in place, it got louder — the howlers were coming in his direction!

He quickly got himself up into a tree — but not just any tree. As a precaution, he went some distance to reach a hemlock on the other side of the creek, that stood where two well–trodden deer trails crossed. He hoped that the deer scent on the trails would keep the howlers off his own scent. And if it didn't, then he'd be able to run from them faster on the deer trails than across unbroken snow.

Not long after he got up into the hemlock the bear came running by, passing under the tree. It went along one of the deer trails, to be able to run faster, but it was soon followed by a pack of howlers. They chased the bear like a pack of wolves would, except that instead of pursuing the bear steadily and silently, they ran flat out, fast and noisy. Tek was thinking about how stupid it was for them to waste so much energy with their unnecessary speed and noise, but he also marveled at how fast some of the younger howlers in the pack were.

The howlers were followed by Others — all men and older boys, some of them carrying long sticks. They were noisy too — shouting excitedly to each other, though nearly breathless, going as fast as they could in the direction of the howlers' noise. Not long after they passed under his tree they stopped and went silent. Like Tek, they knew from the sound of the howlers' noise that the howlers were no longer going away from them, but were instead coming back around toward them.

Tek knew why — the bear must have switched to a different deer trail, one that swung up the slope and then back around, crossing the first trail under his tree. Before long he heard the faint but obvious noise of the approaching bear, running along the second trail in his direction, with the howlers not far behind.

Suddenly there were two claps of thunder and flashes of lightning from where the Others were standing, and then there was no more sound of an approaching bear.

Tek nearly fell out of the tree, from the sudden and unexpected flashes and explosions. He was so frightened that he could not think; he could only keep himself rigid with his claws hooked into the tree's bark. Through the branches he saw that the bear lay still, a black smudge on the snow. Then the howlers reached it and bit and tore at it. One of the Others ran up, clambering through the snow, and pointed his long stick over the heads of the churning howlers. Suddenly there was another flash of lightning and clap of thunder, and this time Tek saw that the thunder and lightning came out of one end of the Other's long stick!

Earlier, the Others' thunder and lightning had killed the bear, but now it only startled the howlers, though that was enough for the Others to rush in and pull them off the bear, cuffing them and shouting roughly at them. The howlers completely subjugated themselves to the Others. They whined and yipped, but they stayed off the bear, distracting themselves by fighting with each other and by casting about, sniffing at scents.

A few of the Others used sharp tools to cut down two saplings, while two of the Others knelt and cut at the bear. From the fighting that then erupted among the howlers, Tek guessed that the Others were throwing pieces of the bear's guts to them.

Now the howlers seemed uninterested in pursuing any other prey, or in making their strident noise. Still, Tek was grateful for the light breeze that carried his scent away from where the Others and their howlers were milling around the bear.

There was an efficiency in everything the Others did. This was not a novel event for them, as it was for Tek. They lashed the bear to their sapling poles, shouldered the poles and left. The howlers followed in an eager procession, fighting among themselves to be among the first behind the Others. Tek thought that the howlers debased themselves, as if they were silly children, instead of the powerful, independent hunters that they were capable of being.

As the forest quieted, Tek's disordered mind gradually settled along with it. Eventually he climbed down the tree and went to where the bear had fallen. Some of its blood was left in the snow, and a few small pieces of innards were strewn around. But the howlers had chewed through most of the bloody snow, and they had picked over the offal so thoroughly, there was hardly anything left for him to scavenge.

As Tek returned to the old woman's home, he tried to absorb the significance of what he had just witnessed.

The Others had seemed so ordinary to him — there were differences, certainly, between them and his own People. For one thing, they had much better tools. But underneath they had seemed to him to be more the same than different. Now he saw, though, that the enormity of his ignorance about them could have easily cost him his life.

Those long sticks of theirs had such strong magic in them — so strong that they could control thunder and lightning spirits! And their power over the howlers — he wouldn't have believed it if he had not seen it with his own eyes. Besides using the howlers to keep forest creatures well away from their homes and belongings, the Others also used them to make their hunting easy. The howlers chased the prey down for them but then — perhaps the magic sticks had something to do with it — the howlers let the Others take the prime meat away from them, leaving them only the innards to fight over.

The howlers were stronger than the Others, but they acted as if they weren't. They seemed to think that they *had* to obey the Others. Tek did not understand the why of that bondage, but he easily understood the danger that it posed to him. If the Others ever decided to hunt him down, they were going to be a much more formidable enemy than he had previously thought.

It also surprised him that the Others handled their magic sticks so casually, as if there was nothing special about them, and that they cuffed their howlers so confidently, as if they had no fear of them at all.

The night was nearly silent as Tek crept into the bess's living space, and climbed to his overhead lair. Before settling himself in for some rest he looked through the gap into the old woman's space. There was something in particular he was looking for.

On previous days in better light, he had noticed a long, thick stick that the old woman had. She kept it propped beside her sleeping place at night, and she hung it in the stonework above her fire pit during the day. Now he could just barely see it in the darkness, leaning against the wall. He had thought it was some kind of staff, but he had never seen her use it to aid her walking. Now he compared it to the magic sticks of the Others he had seen earlier that night: her stick was about the same size and shape as theirs.

After that night Tek kept a greater distance between himself and the two other places where Others dwelt in the valley. And he covered his trail much more carefully whenever he heard the howlers' noise, just in case they might be out hunting with their Others.

Occasionally at dusk or in the early morning light, Tek observed Others as they went along a wide path that went through the valley. The path generally followed the course of the river, but it was a fair distance inland from it. Sometimes the Others had a howler or two with them as they went along this path, or a beast that looked much more like a moose than the bess did — except none of the males had antlers like a moose. Like the bess and the howlers, this beast also acted as if it had to obey the Others. Tek called these beasts 'strapped moose', because when he saw them they always had leather straps all around their heads, that were used to control them.

At times the Others actually rode on the backs of these strapped moose. Other times they made them pull a sled, or an ingenuous wooden box that seemed to float effortlessly above four large spinning hoops. At first Tek thought that those spinning hoops were magic too, until he saw one of them break apart. He watched as the hoop was taken off the box and a rough repair was made to it, enough for the box to be rolled slowly back to where it had been coming from.

Chapter 4

One morning Tek was roused from sleep by a voice, calling from outside the old woman's home. Through the gap in the wood wall, he watched and listened to what went on in the room below.

The old woman opened her front door and stood in her doorway. She was handed a small bundle, which she put on a shelf beside the door, and then from under the shelf she took up a sack full of the sticks she had wound with the strands of fluff. It seemed to Tek that she was trying to block the doorway with her body, but as she leaned to give the sack to someone standing outside, another person shoved past her and entered her home.

The intruder was a large, tall young woman with a commanding presence. She looked and moved around boldly, talking incessantly in a bright, chirping voice. Tek could not understand her words, but he instinctively thought they sounded false.

The old woman watched the young chirping one with a sour expression, occasionally replying with a few curt words. Meanwhile the other visitor, who had stayed outside, returned to the doorway with a large bulging sack. The chirping young woman, with a complete change of tone, spoke brusquely, and the other visitor brought the sack inside.

Though both of the visitors were bundled up in winter clothing, once the second visitor came inside Tek could see that it was a small–featured young woman — hardly more than a girl — who looked like she was . . . one of the People!

The skin of her face and hands was tawny like it was supposed to be, and her hair and eyes were properly dark. Tek could not detect in her the scent that he associated with the People, but because of her presence he was suddenly very interested in every aspect of what went on below.

Though the girl was small and spare, her movements were brisk and she wielded the large sack as if its bulk and weight did not trouble her at all. She did not speak; she watched both the old woman and the young talkative one, particularly the young one. Her gaze was intelligent, but wary.

Her face was scarred all over with splotches, as if at some time in the past, it had been showered with embers from a fire. She was thin and ragged, much like the old woman. In contrast, the brash young woman was plump, early gravid, and wore clothes that looked much fuller and newer.

While the large young woman talked incessantly, she moved around the room, picking up and examining things, going through the old woman's belongings with a seeming idleness, a restless energy. Tek noticed that the old woman spared no attention for the thin girl; instead she followed the roaming young woman, watching her closely. By the expression on her face and her short responses, Tek surmised that she did not trust the young woman, and that she resented the way the young woman was looking through her things.

Twice in her roaming the young woman picked up a short knife with a particularly good handle. It was one that the old woman used a lot, and was probably one of her better tools.

The second time the young woman picked it up, Tek saw that she intended to steal it. She tried to distract the old woman, while positioning the knife to slip it up her sleeve. But the old woman was not fooled. She kept her attention riveted on the young woman, speaking a few tense words and holding out her hand for the knife.

The young woman looked at the old one blankly, and then handed her the knife with a short, barking laugh. She handed it over so carelessly that the old woman had to deftly twist her hand around to its handle, to avoid being cut by it.

The young woman spoke abruptly to the girl, and the girl left. The young woman followed the girl out, deliberately knocking the small bundle they had brought off the shelf, as she left.

The old woman took some deep breaths and moved slowly to the doorway. She stood there for a while, apparently waiting while her visitors left. When all was quiet outside, Tek watched as she knelt slowly to retrieve the bundle, closing the door as she got up with it.

She crossed to her table and opened the bundle. Inside were tightly packed layers of a brown, shriveled substance. The scent from the bundle, wafting up to Tek, was of dried, preserved bear meat that had gone off.

The expression on the woman's face darkened, and she gave a snort of disgust as she sniffed at the top layer. But then she stilled, and peeled back a corner of the top layer. That layer was thin, and there was a coating below it. Scraping some of the coating off and sniffing below it, her expression relaxed and she gave a small nod and a sigh.

With her small knife she carefully scraped off the top layer of meat and the coating, re–wrapped the bundle, and put it with her supply of chilled food.

Tek slipped outside and followed the old woman's visitors. They went back along the long, winding path that went from the old woman's home, to the wide path through the area. He caught up with them on the wide path and followed them at a safe distance.

The young woman was riding one of the beasts that Tek dubbed a 'strapped moose'. A light pole sled dragged along behind it. The sled was two long poles with some cross pieces lashed between them at the back end for a stretched hide platform; the other ends of each pole were strapped to either side of the animal's flanks. The sack of wound sticks that the visitors had collected from the old woman was tied onto the hide platform.

The young woman spoke and laughed a few times, but it seemed to Tek that she was talking to herself. She paid no attention to the girl who followed her silently on foot.

Tek went with them until they turned off onto a path that led to the largest clearing in the valley. The breeze was from the hills that day, and he did not want to rouse the howlers at that location by his scent.

* * *

Riding the cob home from Old Phoebe's hut, Carrie Tutner was well pleased with herself. In an excess of good spirits, she amused herself by mimicking and elaborating on Old Phoebe's curt responses, practicing until she got the clipped tone just right, and chuckling over her cleverness. She was an excellent mimic, partly from natural ability and partly because she practiced whenever the accents did not come easily. She was proud of her skill, and often entertained her family with her pert, irreverent impersonations.

She hadn't managed to snatch that nice little knife of Phoebe's today, but — no matter. It was going to be hers soon anyway. It was practically the only thing that Phoebe had left that was worth anything, other than her land. Even her cow was one of three that rotated to her from her father's herd every year, based on some longstanding arrangement that Carrie had never bothered to fully understand. All of Phoebe's linens were threadbare, and her pots, bowls and platters were chipped, cracked or rusted. Even her musket was rusty, and its stock worm eaten. It would probably blow up in Phoebe's face if she ever tried to fire it. And that would be just fine with Carrie if it did. It would save her the wait.

She did not care a whit that the old woman despised her. Whether the old woman liked it or not, Carrie was going to get everything she owned when she died. Carrie's father had promised it all to her.

Her father was Old Phoebe's closest living relative. Absent a Will, he would inherit all of her property when she died. But to clinch his inheritance, he had long since concocted a Will for her which left her property to him. They would all swear, when the time came, that it was written in Old Phoebe's hand.

He had promised to settle the old woman's property on Carrie, as his eldest and favorite daughter, so that she could marry well, both for her own sake and to enhance the family's standing.

Carrie's brother Sedric was older, but Sedric was to have the parental homestead as his own, someday. Carrie's other brothers and sisters were the children of her father's second wife, and were much younger. Carrie saw to it that none of them came anywhere close to usurping her favored status with their father. When the time came for them, they would have to fend for themselves.

On many a winter's night, Carrie had sat up with her father by their hearth fire, engrossed in discussing Phoebe's withered family bough, and their fine plans for restoring her overgrown homestead, as soon as the old woman was dead and gone. The brushy fields would be cleared. The hovel she lived in would be torn down. A fine new house and barn would be built for the benefit of Carrie and the fortunate young man who would marry her.

Only one thing could upset their rosy plans — if the old woman in her dotage executed a Will of her own, in someone else's favor. So for many years, the family had been careful to interpose itself between the old woman and everyone else, particularly between her and the Klurs — the other family that lived in the valley.

Carrie was now sixteen, and ripe for marriage. Ever since she turned twelve, one of her chores was to keep watch over Phoebe. She did this mainly on visits to Phoebe's hovel, when spun yarns and threads were collected from the old woman, and more raw wool or flax was left with her for spinning. On each visit Carrie searched thoroughly, alert for any change — any detail — that might hint at an upset to their plans.

For four years it had been a rather dull and easy watch. The old woman seemed to tolerate the Tutner family's expectation well enough, and the Klurs did not interfere with the arrangements between the Tutners and their elderly relative. As for the shabby itinerants who sometimes passed through the valley — most of them did not realize that the overgrown path to Phoebe's hut led to a place where anyone still lived. And Phoebe was naturally leery of the few that did venture past her hut.

Four long years . . . the tedious chore of watching over Phoebe had gone on longer than Carrie would have liked. The old woman had been altogether too hale and hardy. But at long last, there were clear signs that the wait was nearly over. There was the shrunken flesh, and the skin unnaturally pale and grey. The slow, careful walk. The shallow breathing. It all meant a rapidly failing heart.

Carrie had seen it before, preceding the death of one of her grandfathers. Oh, yes, Old Phoebe was going to die quite soon, probably within a month.

The timing suited Carrie exceptionally well, because she could no longer afford to wait much longer for Phoebe's land to come to her as her marriage portion. For Carrie had recently discovered that she was pregnant.

The young man she planned to marry was a farmer's son in the next valley over; she wanted him because of his brawn and farming skills. It did not matter that he was probably not the father of the child in her womb. She had slept with him close enough to the right time, to convince him that he was.

But he was adamant: he would not marry her unless a decent farm property was included in the bargain. Carrie had assured him that her marriage portion — Phoebe's farm land — would be hers in time for them to marry over the summer, before the baby was born in the fall.

Childbirth was never a sure thing, but Carrie and her young man knew that pregnancies which made marriage needful, were the ones most likely to come to term.

Working backward from when the birth was expected, Carrie resolved that if Phoebe did not die naturally within the next few weeks, then a quiet but unnatural death awaited her.

Yes, everything was going to fall into place to assure her future happiness, as long as Phoebe was dead within the month, one way or the other.

In her daydreaming Carrie shifted over to detailing her new life as the mistress of her very own home. She knew which of the livestock she would take with her — some of the best cows and the finest bull, and the pick of the sheep, goats, poultry and dogs.

She would take at least two farmhands — the slave Caleb and the indian girl Nika. Caleb would work mostly under her husband, of course, but Nika would be entirely Carrie's. Carrie would no longer have to share her with anyone else.

Carrie wanted Nika because the girl was one of their best workers. But there was also a stubborn pride in Nika, that irritated Carrie. Carrie looked forward to eliminating that, once she had the girl all to herself.

Now in her imaginings Carrie put everything into motion on the rejuvenated homestead. Everything would run smoothly until — perhaps in as little as four or five years — the homestead would be a valuable farm. Then she would arrange for her husband to have a tragic accident.

She already had a few ideas for his timely demise. Perhaps she would arrange for him to be trampled by the bull, or to fall on his head from the barn loft.

Then Carrie in her tasteful widow's weeds would sell the property, and begin a new life of ease in a large city — perhaps one of the great cities of the Atlantic, which her aunt in the port town across the river had told her so much about.

Such were Carrie's castles in the air. She would do her stint as a farmwife, but only as the means to an end, which was to be a comfortably well–off lady in a city that was large enough for an exciting, varied life.

She did not return to the present until they reached her family's dooryard. She turned in the saddle to give instructions to Nika. But before she had a chance to speak, her brother Sedric came charging out of the main barn, bristling as usual with self–importance.

Two years older than Carrie, Sedric had become an ox of a man. Tall and nearly twice as wide as most young men his age, he was fully as strong as he looked.

"I be taking Nika," he announced.

"You'll not!" Carrie countered. "She's still got plenty to do for me."

"I be taking her," Sedric insisted, "because Mickie can't go, and that be your fault. Nika will have to take his place."

"That clumsy oaf! I take no blame for his —"

"Your proddings were the cause of his fall from the ladder."

"Like as not he tripped himself up a purpose," Carrie groused.

"He be laid up because of you," Sedric growled, "and the others that could take his place are gone off with father. I'm needing at least two for getting the logs off the hill. I've got Caleb, and Nika'll have to do as the second. She's the only one of the girls that's strong enough. With my help, we'll manage well enough."

The slave Caleb led a large mule out into the yard, already harnessed to the logging sled. Sedric turned to Nika. "You're coming with me. On to the sled with you." He looked back up at his sister with his most stubborn glare.

Carrie knew that look only too well. It meant that he was not going to back down. When they were younger they would have brawled about it. But Sedric was now much too big and strong; besides, brawling with him was not ladylike. If she wanted to win this fight, her only recourse was to involve their stepmother Constance in it, and to harry her into ruling against Sedric.

Abruptly, Carrie chose to forego this battle. Sedric did not know how soon she was going to have both Caleb and Nika, along with her very own farm property. Then he would be powerless to disrupt whatever plans she made for the use of their time.

But it would not do, to give in too quickly.

"You win this time," she said sourly. "But first Nika must unload the sledge, and the horse must be stabled and watered. *And* you must send her to me as soon as you get back. I've much for her to do." To forestall an argument about *that*, Carrie slid off the horse and stomped into the house without looking back. Once inside, she watched from behind a window curtain as Sedric harried Nika and Caleb to be quick about the work before they left.

*   *   *

On that particular morning Sedric was intent on getting some fir logs down from the hills. The ones he was after had been cut down and loped the preceding week. They were all from trees about twenty years old — just the right size for sawing up. He expected to make a good profit on them, as soon as he got them down from the hill, and over to the sawmill two valleys to the east.

His father had counseled him to wait until the thaw ended and the ground firmed back up, but Sedric chaffed at his father's overcautious advice. He had promised to deliver most of the logs to the sawmill by tomorrow. If he delayed, he would lose standing with the sawyer. And there might be another big snow, or another thaw, delaying him even further. Today was the day for it.

But he was off to a late start because of Carrie.

It made him so angry — the airs his bossy sister had been putting on lately. And she hadn't even *needed* to take a servant with her to Old Phoebe's — she was perfectly capable of fetching the spun wool by herself. But she had snagged Nika and gone off before he'd been properly up and about. How he had fumed, waiting for her to get back, thinking about how fat she was getting, and about her riding around the valley as if she was a great lady, instead of the farmer's daughter that she was. She took all the time in the world and did nothing very useful, while delaying his important, essential work.

When Sedric finally had both Caleb and Nika to himself, he tried to make up the lost time. He hurried them both onto the sled and set off for the hills at a reckless pace, which he was able to maintain well enough until they reached the snowbound slope that went up to his family's woodlot in the hills. Then the going got much slower. They had to break a new path for the sled through wet, mushy snow on the slope. The mule often slipped and floundered, and the heavy sled rocked and shimmied on the curves. It was rough going, and it took them much longer to reach the woodlot than Sedric had planned for.

Once there, for the most part Sedric's job was to exhort, while Caleb and Nika did the lifting and carrying. He harried them while they fetched the logs to the sled, and loaded them on. Though Nika was small and only a girl, she was a lot stronger than she looked and she did at least as much work as Caleb — probably more, Sedric thought, than Mickie would have done. And she worked smart. She leveraged her strength, until it was nearly as effective as Caleb's. The two of them made an odd, but efficient work pair.

The slave and servant put their backs into it, and worked as quickly as Sedric could expect, but it was not going to be enough. Between the late start and the slowness of their long journey up the hillside, Sedric judged that there was only going to be enough time today for one load, instead of the two that he'd counted on. He would not have enough logs to fulfill his promise to the sawyer. His plans were spoiled. And it was all Carrie's fault.

But then, Sedric thought, it was actually more his father's fault than Carrie's — though the late start caused by Carrie had not helped. The real impediment was his father's strict rule, that this sled should never loaded above the tops of its side posts.

Sedric had never questioned that rule before, but now in his stymied, restless state he got up and tromped around the sled, eyeing the load and deciding that his father's rule was, like the old man himself, hopelessly stodgy. The sled was old but sturdy. Sedric judged that it could easily carry twice the load, which would neatly solve his problem.

When Caleb and Nika arrived with what they thought was the last log for this load, Sedric ordered them to bring more. And then more. They got a dozen more logs onto the sled, clambering up to stack them on top of the others. When Sedric finally told them to stop, the sled held nearly a double load.

Surprised glances had passed between Caleb and Nika while they put the additional logs onto the sled. Sedric ignored that and their long faces. He assumed they were sulking about the extra work. But toward the end of the loading, Nika gave the sled a long look, and then stared directly at Sedric. Though she said nothing, her gaze nettled Sedric.

"I'm in charge here," he told her.

Nika could only shrug and look away.

The load was much bigger than normal and they hadn't brought extra rope, so they ran short of rope for lashing the logs down. Instead of four ropes over the load, there were only two.

Sedric took the reins for the trip down, telling Caleb and Nika to squeeze onto the low bench on either side of him. They started out at a slow pace, but Sedric soon increased it because the slope was not very steep at first.

Soon after the increase in speed, the load behind them rose slightly as the sled ran over some unevenness. When it came back down the sled shuddered, and picked up some speed.

Nika spoke up, her voice taut. "Slow it down, Sed! And let us put the slowing stakes down. If we don't we're sure to crash!"

At first Sedric was too amazed to reply. The chit had never, *ever* spoken to him like that before! He had lately been thinking that the quiet, hard–working girl was secretly — and hopelessly of course — sweet on him. Now he saw he'd been wrong. She was nothing but an uppity, interfering female, just like all the others, and she had just overstepped her low place.

"I know what I'm doing!" he snapped, giving the reins a slap.

But he soon lost his assurance. The slope had only steepened slightly, but the sled was gaining too much speed. Soon the slope would be even steeper, and there was a sharp curve ahead.

Sedric was very strong and he pulled the reins hard, but the overloaded sled rushed the mule forward. He ordered Caleb and Nika to lower the slowing stakes. They got them both jammed down, but it was too late. The stakes only raked through the wet snow and mud, their friction making little difference against the gathering momentum of the overloaded sled.

"Just look at this mess you've got us into, Nika!" Sedric yelled, as he realized that at the very least there was going to be a messy accident.

And then, "Bail!" he screamed, as the sled lifted and shimmied, gaining ever more speed.

Caleb jumped off one side immediately, and Sedric followed him. But Nika did not jump.

She slid over and grabbed the reins before they fell out of reach.

She did not do it because Sedric had unfairly blamed her, or because she thought she could prevent the accident. She knew sled probably *was* going to crash. But she thought that the mule deserved that she should try to save it. After the curve that was coming up, the path leveled off for some distance. If she could slow the sled enough to ease it around the curve, then she might be able to keep the sled from running over the mule.

She tried to slow the sled by steering the mule to one side of the track, into untrodden snow. But the mule was feeling too much crowding. It kept veering back onto the track, where it was easier for it to stay ahead of the sled. Nika battled with the mule's will, steering the sled more and more desperately in a rocking, sliding zig zag across the downward sloping track.

They gained ever more speed. The sled went airborne for a few sickening moments over a bump, and when it came down the load of logs behind Safa shifted. The sled gave a heavy, sharp jerk, snapping the mule's harness on one side. The mule was violently jostled and nearly thrown off its feet, but it was still strapped to the sled, and the curve loomed ahead.

Suddenly the mule understood that it was in peril of being run over. It let out a frightened squeal and clove to the track to outrun the load, nearly galloping. It had panicked, but was not quite out of its mind yet. Nika strained back on the reins, pulling as hard as she could to get the mule off the track once again.

But the last moment for control had passed. The front of the gaining sled veered and whacked the backs of the mule's flying hooves. The mule completely lost its head, galloping straight down the track. The sled gained speed and overtook the mule in the curve.

As the sled ran over the screaming mule Nika threw herself off the sled, toward the inside of the curving track. One of the jostling, loosened logs on the sled hit her ankle as it whizzed past, violently jerking and somersaulting her airborne body. The sled rolled sideways toward the outer side of the curve, spewing logs and dragging and rolling the crushed mule. Logs bounced and flew in all directions, some fantastically end over end, but most in wild, bucking rolls down and across the track, and into trees.

As the sled roared past Nika she was conscious of being spun in the air for a few moments, and in those instants she so wished that she really was a bird, like she sometimes dreamed about being. A bird could just fly away from this. Instead, she was going to be slammed into scrub or a tree.

Fragments of her life flashed before her. Orphaned at age eight, she had striven mightily through the six years since then, under indenture to the Tutners. She had worked so hard and long, determined to wrest respect from the family, despite the many proofs that they were forever hardened against her. Why she had continued to labor with such will for them, she herself did not know, except that it stemmed from a belief in her worth as a person, that she always tried to live up to. She had thought that as long as she retained this sense of herself, everything would somehow work out alright for her in the end.

But now came an illuminating moment, when she saw that all she had done to keep her dignity intact — was going to be for naught. Even if she survived, Sedric was going to blame her for this accident. She was going to be the lowly servant who was to blame for the dead mule, the destroyed sled, and likely for her own death as well.

Her soul cried out that it was not fair or right. But by everything that life had taught her, she knew that it would be so.

* * *

After jumping off the sled, Sedric and Caleb both ran down after it. Caleb got to where it crashed first. He had time, before Sedric arrived, to ascertain that Nika, oddly twisted and still in the snow near the base of a large tree, was dead, and that the mule, crushed but still alive and groaning in agony, needed to be put out of its misery. Caleb had an axe on his belt, but he could not use it to end the mule's life. As a slave, he had to first get the permission of his master's son.

He shrugged his jacket off and put it over the indian girl splayed in the snow. His patched and threadbare garment could be of no conceivable use to her now. But it was his tribute to the wretched girl who had toiled alongside him, sometimes even — inexplicably — taking a share of his work onto her own thin shoulders. He was truly sorry, that it had ended for her like this.

He remembered his first glimpse of her when she arrived six years ago. He'd been crossing the dooryard when the big wagon pulled in, back from carrying harvested grain to the port town across the river. He looked up and saw the little waif, with her pockmarked face, perched on the wagon's high bench. It was a given that she was an orphan, a court's ward that the master had taken on at almost no cost to himself.

In her first years with them he had watched her morosely, patient for the day that would surely come, when her drive would slacken and her spirit sag, from her realization that the Tutners' indentured servants would never do any better in life than their slaves. The length of their terms was too long, the work too harsh, and the fare too meager. There were too many ways for the Tutners to wring everything out of them before their terms expired.

Caleb knew that Nika had come to know all this — certainly she had known by the end of the first year. But strangely she had *not* slackened in her work, and her spirit had *not* been broken by the stark realities. Year then followed year. The girl stubbornly continued to delude herself, but even so Caleb came to prize the fleeting, conspiratorial smile that she sometimes gave him when they were both certain that no one else would see it. By degrees it kept alive in him a hope that somehow this small but tough, birdlike indian girl was going to find a way to escape the cage of servitude that confined them both.

But not like this — not by death. He had never wanted her escape in this way, sprawled lifeless on a snowy hillside.

Caleb knew Nika well enough to know why she had stayed on the sled. As sure as the sun rose in the morning, she'd been trying to save that miserable mule, thinking that, if she couldn't, she would still be able to jump clear in time. But she had misjudged, or had just been unlucky, and this was the sad end of it.

Caleb wondered at how deeply her death was sorrowing him, and at how much it hurt him for his small hope for her to be dashed. He had been right all along, but he took no satisfaction from that. A last wave of sorrow washed through him, nourishing his humanity. All too soon he would harden his heart against everyone and everything again, this time without exception.

When Sedric reached the place of the accident, Caleb had difficulty getting him to give the order that plainly needed to be given, to end the mule's suffering. At first Sedric could not give the mule any thought, being fully engaged in working out the best way to direct all blame for the accident onto the dead girl. But when the mule's plaintive whinnies and groans at last disturbed the flow of his frantic thoughts, he ordered Caleb to axe it.

As soon as that was done, they started down the steep hill to get some help. All the way down Sedric coached Caleb on his version of the accident.

In it, the sled had *not* been overloaded, and the girl was alone at the reins from the outset. Sedric and Caleb had been on either side of the mule's head, guiding it down the slope slowly — Sedric emphasized how very slowly. Then, either from impatience or as some kind of foolish joke, the stupid girl had slapped the reins on the mule's back, and that was all it took. When the mule jolted ahead, he and Caleb had to jump aside, out of the way. From then on, the crash was inevitable.

"And you'll remember that I told the fool girl to take it real slow down the mountain, won't you, Caleb?" Sedric asked.

Caleb mumbled some words that could be taken as agreement.

He was a survivor. He knew better than to contradict the master's son. Masters and masters' sons always blamed the servants and the slaves for the accidents. Servants first, usually, to increase their indentures if they survived the accident.

Caleb shrewdly knew that Nika would have been quite upset about being blamed, if she had lived. But he himself was a complete realist. And besides, the truth did not matter to Caleb because it could not bring his friend Nika back.

*　*　*

Sedric had hoped to involve only his own family in the aftermath of the accident, but on his way home with Caleb they met the Klur family on the road. Old man Klur and his two daughters had also been out harvesting one of their woodlots, though on a much more modest scale, and for their own use.

The old man stopped to watch Sedric and Caleb approach, and when they reached him he asked Sedric what was wrong. He knew just by looking at the two of them that something bad had happened.

Thus the Klurs learned about the accident, and that the mule and the indian girl were dead.

"You be certain the girl's dead?" the old man asked.

When Sedric did not reply, Caleb did. "She looked it," he stated glumly. "No movin' t'all. Neck twisted near full around. Limbs be ever which a way."

Sedric hurriedly assured old Klur that they didn't need any neighborly help, even though Klur had not offered any.

As soon as Sedric and Caleb were far enough away on their way home, the old man unhitched his mule from their sled. He sent his younger daughter Hannah back home to get their other mule, for dragging their sled the rest of the way home. He and his older daughter Ruth went up the hill with the mule they had with them, to see if there was anything they could do for the indian girl.

The old man did not particularly care for indians, having lost his wife and an infant son in one of the last of their terrible raids through the area, nearly twenty years earlier. But Nika was different. She was still hardly more than a child, and he had heard tell that she was a Christian. But more important to him, and unbeknownst to everyone but the Klurs themselves, she had earned his family's respect, for a quiet act of kindness.

A few springs previous, the younger Klur daughter had a bout of severe headaches, which none of their remedies abated. Nika was in the Tutners' dooryard when Ruth came to ask Carrie for some lavender oil, which she promised to replenish after they procured some on their next trip to the river town. But Carrie turned Ruth away, telling her that they had none of the precious oil to spare.

On Ruth's way home, Nika caught up with her and asked if they had tried a tea made from willow bark. They had not known of it, so Nika took Ruth to a stand of white willow and showed her how to peel the bark from the young, brightly-colored branches. She gave her instructions for drying the bark and preparing the tea. The willow tea lessened the headaches, as nothing else had.

When Klur and Ruth reached the accident place, they found Nika much as Caleb said she would be, except she wasn't dead, at least not yet. She was senseless though, as they checked her over and carefully lifted her and lashed her to their mule's back.

Neither the old man nor Ruth gave the girl very good odds for recovering.

Before they left they looked over the site. It was not from idle curiosity. As much as possible they judged character from their own observations, rather than from what they were told.

They gauged from what they saw that the sled had been grossly overloaded, and the logs inadequately secured. They observed the splintered drag stakes, and the veering zig zag cuts across the path, leading into the curve. Ruth labored further up the hill by herself; when she returned she told her father that she had found the place where Caleb and Sedric had jumped off the same side of the sled.

So it was not at all as Sedric had told them. They knew where the blame for the accident really lay — with Sedric.

As Klur and his daughter labored down the slope with their mule and its small, light burden, Klur thought about the likely fate of this indian girl, if he delivered her to the care of the Tutner family.

He suspected that the brash and grasping family would rather have her back dead, than alive. Alive — she would need a lot of care that they would find burdensome, and then — if she recovered — would she be too maimed to have any value as a servant? She also might have something inconvenient to say of the accident, that would not agree with Sedric's version. Dead — it would be much simpler for them, and far less trouble.

Klur turned over in his mind whether he had any duty, or inclination, to give the girl a somewhat better chance.

He found no duty, but he did have an inclination.

It did not seem right to him to leave the girl's recovery to the questionable care and mercy of the Tutners. And Sedric's self–serving lies had nettled him. Klur had never thought much of him. The boy — now a half–formed young man — had always tended toward rash bullying, and blaming others for his own mistakes. Some such youths eventually changed for the better, but Klur judged that Sedric was unlikely to be one of that type.

Klur saw that he had two choices, if he did not take the girl to the Tutners. He could have his own family care for her, or he could ask Old Phoebe if she would be willing to do it.

He did not think that the Tutners would tolerate his own family's care of their servant for very long — they would view it as meddling in their affairs. They would soon fetch the girl away, with irritated expressions of false gratitude — probably within a few days.

But if Old Phoebe took her in . . . the Tutners might actually allow that, since Phoebe was related to them, and it would be much less trouble for them, to have Phoebe care for her. He knew that Phoebe thought well of the girl, as he and his family did. He saw no harm in asking her if she was wont to get involved.

Before he spoke of it with his daughter Ruth, he wondered if her thoughts were running in the same direction as his, as they often did.

Daily in his prayers he thanked his Maker for this daughter. She was plain and somewhat clumsy, and well past the best marrying age. But in his heart, she would always be the plucky child that had found her way back to him through the vast wilderness, when she was only nine years old.

The raiding indians had taken some of his scalp and left him for dead, and had taken his wife and children away with them. But Ruth had not been tied as securely as the others, and she had gotten away from their captors, as they continued their raiding through other valleys. His wife and infant son had been found dead, farther up alongside the indian trail to Canada. His daughter Hannah was later found in Montreal, and was bought out of her servitude there.

He knew that even after all these years, his Ruth still sorrowed that she had left her mother and siblings with their captors. But her mother had been wild for her to take her chance to run off into the woods, and to find her way back home to him.

Now, Klur simply asked her, "What do you think?"

And without a pause to ask him what he meant or to consider further she answered, "Let's take her to Phoebe."

Chapter 5

As the day's light was fading, Tek's rest was disturbed by another unusual stir of activity in the old woman's home. More visitors had arrived. This time it was a man somewhat past his prime, and a full-grown woman. They resembled each other; Tek guessed they were related — perhaps a father and daughter. And he recognized where they were from by their scents: they occupied the smaller of the two other clearings in the valley.

The visitors spoke gravely with the old woman, with a deliberateness — an intensity — which was taken up in the tone of her voice when she responded. This was not an ordinary kind of visit. Something serious was being decided.

After some conversation they all went outside, leaving the door open. They soon returned carrying hemlock boughs, which they layered up in front of the hearth, followed by balsam boughs which they put crossways over the hemlock. One of Phoebe's hides was laid over it all, and they carried in the girl that had visited earlier that day — the one that Tek thought was one of the People. But there was something seriously wrong with her now.

She was injured — bruised, limp, and unnaturally still — so different from when he had last seen her. She did not awaken while the old woman and the woman visitor worked over her.

The old man, who had helped carry the girl in, took a quick look around, and then busied himself outside. Before long he brought in several armfuls of wood, and got a good fire going in the hearth.

The visitors left soon after, but they both came back later, after dark. This time they brought some baskets and bundles of food, and a lot of wood that they stacked up mostly in the bess's space. Before they left the second time, they also made several trips to the creek, to build up the old woman's supply of water.

It was on one of their trips carrying wood into the bess's space, through the doorway between the old woman's space and the bess's, that the visitor woman stopped suddenly and looked up to where Tek was watching all of the activity below, through the small gap in the wall. She stared so intently and long that Tek was certain she could somehow see him, though he had not made a sound, and it seemed impossible that she could see him through the small gap, in the deep shadows there.

He kept perfectly still, frozen in place by her stare until, just as abruptly as she had stopped and stared, she broke off her gaze and went back to carrying wood into the bess's space. After that, though she never looked up to where he was again, Tek could not shake the feeling that she knew he was up there. For one thing, she began to speak in whispers, as if she thought he might overhear her, and understand what she was saying.

Near the end of all the bustle, the door between the bess's space and the old woman's space was closed, but not latched. The visitors left and the old woman went to bed shortly after that, with the door still not latched. This presented Tek with a rare opportunity to slip inside the old woman's space later on.

* * *

Nika's next awareness was of waking up in Old Phoebe's cold hovel, on some bedding on the floor. It was dark and silent, but she knew where she was by the shapes in the darkness, and by the smell that always pervaded the place, of wood smoke mixed with the herbs the old woman hung about the place.

When she tried to move, pain exploded in her back, neck and arms, and one of her ankles throbbed dully. So she lay still in the darkness, wondering how she came to be here instead of her own bed in the Tutners' attic.

She remembered the accident, and her stomach twisted with knowing she had been blamed for it. But she could not fathom how that had caused her to be lying here, beside Phoebe's cold hearth. She cast back in her mind for an explanation.

* * *

58

Nika had met Old Phoebe for the first time a few weeks after she had arrived in the area, six years earlier. Some hogs had been slaughtered, with one of the smaller heads being put aside for Phoebe. The head was owed to Phoebe for some flax she had spun into thread for the master's wife. But in all the bustle no one took the head to Phoebe until a few days after the slaughtering, when it was noticed because it began to have an off odor. By then even the dogs stopped trying to reach where it swung from a high hook. It was taken down and handed to Nika, with some hasty instruction for the route to Old Phoebe's place.

After going some distance on the better, more travelled roads, Nika turned off onto a winding, overgrown path that was little more than a deer trail. She guessed that it had once been an indian trail as well, because of the way it followed the land, and because it led down to a creek. In the early days of settlement it had probably been one of the main routes through the area, but new roads had long since been cut. Now the old trail petered out in the forest just beyond Phoebe's place, after crossing the creek.

The hasty instructions had Nika turn back when she reached this creek, and to search along the rising ground for the obscured spur path that led to Phoebe's hut, for she was certain to have missed it on her way in.

Nika called out as she lugged the hog's head up to Phoebe's door. After a while there were sounds from inside the hut and the door scraped and creaked open. A scrawny old cat minced out, stretching itself, and then there stood Phoebe framed in the doorway — a tall, thin, wrinkled old woman, staring down at Nika.

The old woman could see what Nika was carrying, and there was nothing the matter with her nose. When Old Phoebe got a whiff of the hog's head, Nika easily read, in the expressions that flitted across her face, that the old woman was annoyed, but not surprised, by the off smell. Clearly, this was not the first time that her relatives had paid her for her flaxwork with something rendered less valuable by their careless ways.

With a hollow cough, Phoebe moved aside and motioned Nika into her hut. The slimy head was deposited onto the cold hearth, and Nika was politely asked to fetch some water from the creek. She was given an old mended bucket for the water, that had not one but two trickle leaks in its worn wooden staves. When she got back with the water she found Phoebe crouched on the hearth digging out the hog's eyes with a short knife, muttering disgustedly about all the difference that a day or two could have made, for pity's sake, if only —

Phoebe broke off when she heard Nika nearby. A fire was started in the hearth; as soon as the fire was going well enough Phoebe sent Nika away, first telling her to be sure to inform her kin that she was in fine fettle and that she wanted for nothing.

When Nika got back to the busy Tutner homestead, she had not expected to be questioned about any aspect of her errand. But it was the master himself who took her aside and questioned her closely about Old Phoebe. Did she look hale or ill? Did she move easy, or did she creep? How was her color — ruddy, or pale?

Nika was hard pressed to answer her new master's questions in a way that was both truthful and within Old Phoebe's stricture. Nika's own assessment was that Phoebe was frail, and just barely over a serious chest ailment. But the old woman wanted Nika to report to her kin that she was well.

Nika reasoned to herself that sometimes the old ones *did* have a surprising resilience . . .

She gave Phoebe the benefit of her doubt. Under her master's barrage of questions, she stated that Phoebe had seemed to be quite ordinary to her. She answered him quickly enough and offhandedly, as if she had neither seen nor heard anything to give rise to the slightest concern.

Her master seemed disappointed with the news he so avidly solicited, but in any case Phoebe confirmed Nika's judgment by showing a remarkable vitality over the ensuing six years. Up until recently, whenever Nika was sent on an errand to Old Phoebe's home, the old woman always seemed much the same — tenaciously maintaining her existence in the small clearing on her land.

Four years ago, Carrie began to accompany Nika on most of the errands to Phoebe's. While Nika performed the work of the errand, Carrie looked around and went through Phoebe's belongings with greedy eyes and fingers. Even a fool could see that Carrie expected to get her old relative's property when she died.

Neither Phoebe nor Nika were fools.

Nika sometimes thought that Carrie's avarice actually increased Phoebe's longevity. It was as if the tough old woman gained some extra measure of strength, if for no better reason than to make Carrie wait as long as possible for what wasn't hers, but was so obviously coveted.

*   *   *

Over the years a tentative, hidden friendship arose between the old woman Phoebe and the girl Nika. Phoebe found that the girl had a pleasant disposition, strength of character, and she also sensed a goodness in Nika that was rare in her experience of human beings. Nika for her part admired the old woman's quiet, uncomplaining resilience, and she responded to what she sensed was the old woman's liking and respect for her.

Neither of them acknowledged the friendship, even between themselves, for there was nothing good to be gained by it. They both knew that the Tutner family would not approve of a friendship between their old kinswoman and anyone beyond their immediate family — least of all, one of their lowly servants.

*   *   *

Lying as still as possible in the darkness of Old Phoebe's hut, Nika still could not think of anything that would explain how she had come to be housed here now. Her mind wandered further, seeking explanation.

She had been indentured here when she was eight, not long after her parents and little brother died of the small pox. She along with them had been stricken by it soon after the four of them arrived at the bustling town across the river, where her father had hoped to get some portage or guide work. The disease was not strong enough to take Nika's life along with theirs, but she was left heavily pocked by it. As an orphan she became a charge on the public until the local court was able to bind her to service for her upkeep. Though she was disfigured by the pocks and quite small for her age, it did not take the court long to find a master for her on one of the outlying farms, which were always short of laborers.

Her new master, Jacob Tutner, had come to the town with a bumper harvest of grain to sell. He was on the lookout for some cheap labor to take back with him — either a slave that he judged was healthy enough despite a low price, or better yet — usually cheaper yet — an orphan that could be indentured. He was in luck: the pox had recently swept through the town, leaving two hardy orphans — a white boy of five years, and an indian girl of eight. Jacob was friendly with the court's clerk — as boys they'd had some schooling together, and thus he got first pick between the two. He chose the indian girl. She was older and thus able to do more work from the outset. And being a careful man, Jacob preferred an indian, confident that he would always prevail if any dispute ever arose over the servant's treatment.

When they arrived back at the Tutner homestead Nika was turned over to her new master's wife, to be taught her place and her work. The Tutner servants and slaves were not pampered: the Tutners excelled at working them to their full capacity, and beyond. Nika learned her work quickly and well, and did it without grumbling or giving trouble. She missed her family terribly, never forgetting her parents' love and teachings. She hardened herself to make the best of her situation in life. She gave the Tutners no just cause for complaint.

Gradually over the years she was trusted with a greater range and amount of work, including men's work when called upon.

She served all of the Tutners, but preferred working under her master Jacob. He drove his workers — as they all did — but he was not usually as relentless as the others.

Sedric was the one that Nika liked least. Soon after she arrived, she sized him up as an arrogant boy with a cowardly heart, and he had done nothing since then to raise himself in her opinion. And he was mercurial — steady enough one day, but cocky and edgy the next.

Carrie and her stepmother could both be vicious, but at least they were predictable. With them it was more a matter of staying out of trouble by seeming to follow their orders and rules conscientiously, no matter how ill–advised some of them were.

Once in a long while, Nika did break their rules. That very morning, Carrie had given her a bundle of spoiled meat to take with them to Phoebe's, as payment for her spinning work. Nika substituted some good meat for it, from what had been brought from the store room, to be soaked for the day's dinner. She did the substitution cleverly, slipping lard and a layer of bad meat on top of the good meat, in case Carrie untied the bundle and checked it.

What had always driven Nika to excel — which only incidentally benefited the Tutners so much, was an innate generosity and hospitality that she felt bound to extend to everyone who did not show themselves unworthy of it. Her generosity compelled her to be patient and helpful with all but those who were cruel in a direct and obvious way.

Reinforced by Christian principles of charity and meekness, learned at her mother's knee, her simple faith had served her well thus far — especially the last six years as a penniless orphan and servant. She had known of no flaw in her principles, according to her own definitions and terms.

But now, lying badly injured in the dark hut — perhaps with permanent injuries and pains that would never fade, Nika's heart told her, and her reason confirmed, that she had been too generous, and it had nearly cost her her life, and was the cause of her present suffering.

She had never judged the Tutners to be cruel — only selfish, uncaring and greedy. Now she saw — with a clarity that came too late, that a less obvious cruelty sprang from heedless, heartless traits — so unlike her own.

She wondered what would have happened if she had refused to take any part in overloading the sled — if she had stopped when she first knew that what Sedric was doing was wrong.

That 'what if' began a series of cascading, meandering 'what ifs', until her head ached worse than ever. She was unconscious for a while, and then she slipped in and out of awareness. Whenever consciousness returned, her stark miscalculation of cruelty bedeviled her, until she made herself put it aside by degrees, to concentrate on surviving the pain.

Several times she had disjointed fragments of dreams. Then she had a more coherent dream that started out like one of the 'owl' dreams she had been having lately. But in this dream, she was not an owl but was instead one of the ancient spirits of her People, like in her father's stories.

Her father had been a wonderful teller of the old stories. In her dream she could almost hear the rise and fall of his husky, mellifluous voice, and could almost see the light in his eyes as he sculpted the spirits out of air, with his words and hands.

In this dream she was flying silent, fast and high above a dark forest that stretched out in the moonlight for as far as she could see — and she could see amazingly far and well. She was floating in the air, absorbing every detail, and so alive and free from pain. Her soul expanded with joy, and her vision was exhilarating, fascinating — so unlike earthbound vision.

Suddenly she convulsed with pain, as something seized her and carried her on large and powerful dark wings. She was a prisoner; she had been tricked in this dream. Her dream knowledge told her that she was an invulnerable sky spirit, but she had only been a small owl after all — and was now caught in the talons of a hawk. If only she had known, if only she had not been tricked — she would have been watchful, and this hawk would never have been able to catch her.

In her dream she struggled to free herself — not just physically but also from the unfairness of being tricked. But the hawk only tightened its grip. She cried out from the pain of the talons in her neck and back, and woke up, heart pounding and gasping for breath.

Nearby in the darkness something stirred.

At first Nika thought it was Phoebe. But the slight sounds and movement had not come from the corner where Phoebe's bed was, and Nika could hear Phoebe's ragged breathing over there, as well. No, the sounds had come from the other side of her pallet, where there was a shape — a deeper darkness in the darkness, that was unmoving now with an unnatural stillness — a stillness that Nika interpreted as a stalking stillness.

Still partly in her dream, Nika felt she had the extraordinary sight and hearing of an owl, and she also had a great fear — a fear that the dark form close by was the hawk from her dream. She tried to shift away from it, but that began a riot of painful throbbings throughout her body. She waited, helpless and barely breathing, for reality to reassert itself.

But the seconds stretched and lengthened. The terrifying dark shape, and her fear of it, did not fade.

She tried to lessen her fear by whispering the words of the Lord's Prayer, in her own language. Her mother had taught her to say this prayer whenever she was most afraid.

* * *

During that night Tek had gone out to hunt, for he was very hungry. But his hunting was not successful. The air was getting colder. A snow was brewing, a big one. He along with the other creatures of the forest could feel it. The bear wind from the north was coming back, lugging with it an exceptionally large and thick snow pelt.

Though the giant spirit's winter home would be melting away before long, he could still be very strong and harsh. And he was fully capable of hurling one of his largest and heaviest snow pelts across the land.

Many of the prey that Tek hunted — the hares, the squirrels, the turkeys and such, had already retreated to their burrows and nests, to sleep through the cold, deep whiteness that was going to bury their food and make it difficult for them to move about as usual.

Tek returned to the old woman's home with an empty stomach. He had already decided to explore her space when he got back, if the door between her space and the bess's was still unlatched. And while he was there, he would try for a mouse or two. The few that were left were all much more cautious of him than when he had first arrived, but tonight he would have an advantage: they would not expect him to be hunting them in the old woman's part of the space, where he had never been before. If the direction of the draft through her space favored him, he just might get one of them.

He slipped into the bess's space, and silently approached the inside door. He eased it slightly open, just enough to squeeze past it. When the door began to creak and scrape, he simply waited for the building to groan in a buffet of wind, to hide the noise.

Once inside the old woman's space, Tek made a methodical search. He was already familiar with most of the scents; mixes of them continually wafted up to the loft in the bess's space where he normally slept. Now he took particular care to scent items separately. He meticulously scented the magic stick that was propped beside the old woman's bed. Up close it did not smell much different from what many of her tools were made from. He smelled the wood of it, and the hard substance that was also part of many of her tools. The only difference was a dull sour odor, with a mix of burnt minerals about it. From offerings, he wondered?

He saved his observation of the girl on the floor for last. He had not been ignoring her. He simply wanted to do everything else first.

While he had been moving silently through the space around the girl, she had shifted a few times in her sleep, and groaned or whimpered quietly. It was obvious that she had been badly hurt and was in a lot of pain, but she did not cry out. Tek knew how hard it was to suffer in silence. He settled down near her, absorbing her scent, and watching and listening to her every movement. The fire was down to a few darkened embers, so it was very dark. But he could see her form in the darkness with his night vision.

She looked to him like she ought to be one of the People, but she had more of the scent of Others about her, than of the People, and that troubled him.

He kept perfectly still, the better to observe her, but also in case his stillness would lull a mouse into venturing forth, far enough away from the safety of its niche in the wall for him to catch it. He was sitting on his haunches, still but ready to pounce.

The girl became agitated in her sleep, and uttered a small cry that sounded eerily like an owl's kweeeek. Tek shifted uncomfortably; the cry reminded him so strongly of a sound made by his brother's wife Tsihi, when she was in her owl shape.

Silence followed, except for the girl's fast and shallow breathing. She was awake now. Tek guessed that she had been dreaming, and that her dream had frightened her. This seemed confirmed when a whimper and groan broke into her ragged breathing.

Neither the People nor the Others had good night vision, so Tek did not think that the girl could see him in the darkness. But her head moved about, as if she could see at least as well as he could in the darkness. Then she stiffened when she came to stare at exactly where he was sitting in the darkness.

Tek held himself stiller than ever.

The girl began to whisper some words.

Tek could not understand many of the words, but some of them seemed familiar. She used words that were something like the words he knew for 'father', for 'sky', and for something like 'living in goodness'.

Each word that he recognized — not quite the same but similar — reverberated in his mind, creating ripples of flowing thoughts. He shivered in the widening, successive waves, with full understanding slipping around the edges of the words, just out of reach.

He had known for some time, that he had died the night of the desperate fight with Okat. But instead of passing on to where the People went after death, he had been held back somehow, as if caught in some swirling eddy of time's river. It could be as meaningless as that — simply caught in a snag as a quirk of nature. But he wondered. What if he had been kept back for some purpose, known only to the spirits of the People.

The girl repeated what she was whispering several times. Each time that he picked out the familiar words for 'father' and 'sky', the ripples of thought from them crossed each other in his mind, in vibrating, undulating flows that seemed to buffet him, bringing up images in his mind of the time he had spent in a cave, with his wounds and his torn, mangled innards being prodded and salved by the huge, scentless bear. He remembered the strange chanting that he heard while he was there — with words similar to those he had known but also not quite the same. None of those words were exactly like words he had heard before or since; it was these little differences that clashed and unsettled his mind now.

But his recollections reinforced his notion that his being here was *not* a fluke — that there *was* some purpose or meaning to it somehow. The great bear spirit had held him back from his after–life journey for some reason. What that reason would be — probably the bear spirit itself did not know with any exactness. Tek sensed strongly that time had moved strangely after the bear spirit's ministrations. He felt so old in his bones, and the scents of so many things were similar but not really the same . . . this, he thought, might be explained by a great passage of time, much greater than the normal aging of a boy, a buck or a lynx.

In the darkness, as the girl's words flowed around and through him like fracturing echoes, Tek returned his attention to her. She was shuddering now, perhaps from the cold. There were some covers over her but, with no warmth from a fire, she probably could not keep herself warm. Her voice was shaky, from pain and cold but also, Tek sensed, because she knew he was there and was afraid of him. She must think that he was there to harm her.

Cautiously Tek crept closer to her, stopping when his face was nearly touching hers. She stopped whispering the words and stared back at him. Tek did not yet understand how she could see his shape in the darkness, but he made a low sound in his throat, meant to reassure her.

*   *   *

Nika watched the dark shape come closer, until she could see what it was. She was relieved that it was not the hawk from her dream.

But . . . it was a lynx. By the scrawny, gaunt look of its terribly scarred face, it was a rather old one. And probably, if it had found its way in here looking for food, it was a very hungry one. And here she was, helpless . . .

She was about to call out to waken Phoebe, when the lynx purred in a rough but unmistakable way. And with the purr she thought she could detect an odd beseeching look in its eyes that was . . . almost human. It was almost as if it wanted to tell her, to not be afraid.

*   *   *

Tek decided that the girl was definitely too cold. He slipped inside the coverlets and laid down with his back against her side, purring quietly.

*   *   *

Nika had not felt the cold much before, but now it was as if it was draining her life away. She was grateful for the warmth from the

68

lynx's body. Together, they would be warmer than either could be separately.

She wondered if the lynx was here because Phoebe had tamed it, and that it actually lived here with her. Phoebe's old cat had died several years ago . . . she had never noticed this lynx around here before, but it would be natural for a half–wild lynx to hide whenever Phoebe had visitors. Gradually Nika relaxed, and began again to slip in and out of consciousness.

*   *   *

Tek lay awake, with memories of his brother's wife Tsihi, and her ability to shape shift into a small owl. She had always been kind to him. He had loved her, and he missed her more than anything else in his past life.

Unexpectedly, he found more reassurance of life, than the sadness of loss, in the remembrances. The hut's darkness became very bright and comforting for him, as it filled with those recollections.

He remembered the countless things, both large and small, that had defined Tsihi's beauty, both spiritually and in her every glance and touch. He remembered her as a person, small but strong, smart and kind. To have been loved by such a person as that, gave him a reassurance that comforted him now, as nothing else could.

In her owl shape, she had helped him get out of the clanhouse, that first time he had shapeshifted to buck. And he had marveled at her outsized owl fierceness, up against the threat of Okat's evil. Small and light and quite fragile, but diving nonetheless at the panther Okat those several times, wings back, eyes fixed and talons aching for grip and blood.

The girl by his side was something like Tsihi had been, as a person. She was small for what he judged her age to be, and though she was injured now, when he had seen her earlier she was strong and quick–minded. And when he stared into her eyes a short while ago, he thought he had seen something of his beloved Tsihi's strengths and kindness inside of her.

And — that kweeeek noise that the girl had made earlier, when she was coming out of her dream. It was so like the sound that a startled owl would make, and so like a sound that Tsihi sometimes made when she was an owl.

Having gotten this far, it did not take a great leap of imagination for Tek to understand why the girl had been able to see him in the darkness. If she was an owl shapeshifter, as Tsihi had been, then she would have an owl's keen night sight and hearing.

Not much later on, when the girl lying beside him shapeshifted into an owl, Tek was not the least bit surprised.

* * *

Nika was having another one of her strange 'owl' dreams.

Before her injuries, they always began the same way, and followed a similar course. She would wake during the night on her straw pallet in the Tutners' attic, as a small owl instead of a girl. She would scramble out from under her thin coverlet, and then savor the night air in the cold room, enjoying her clear sightedness in the darkness, and her sharp crisp hearing. She would listen to the deep, regular breathing of the other female servants who slept in the attic with her, each in turn. When she was certain they all slept soundly, she would flap silently over them, to the window at the east end of the attic that was always left open a hand's breadth. Landing on the sill, she would slip through the opening and take off into the night sky, rising on her wings with a joy of being that was completely at odds with her real life.

She had thought that was what her owl dreams were for — for the joy and wonderment that buoyed her spirits after each dream.

But her present dream would give no buoyant joy. In this dream, she was not on her attic pallet, but was instead on the hide pallet on Phoebe's floor. And sure enough, the pain of her injuries intruded forcefully into her dream.

But her injuries were noticeably less painful than when she had last fallen into sleep as a person. Her last conscious awareness as a person had been that even the slightest movement generated explosive agony. Now in her dream she was able to move about a little, as an owl under the coverlets. Her little owl body still pained her too much for her to scramble out from under it. But she could claw at the coarse fabric with her talons, and struggle to shift her wings against it.

70

Then the coverlets lifted off her, and she could see that a lynx was looming over her in the darkness. It was the same one, inside her dream, that had lain alongside her before she had slept and dreamed. Now in her dream the lynx sniffed her and nuzzled her. Then it rolled her toward it, gathering her up against its belly, and curling its body around her. It settled over her by twisting its neck around, over her head.

Nika did not like being tumbled about by this lynx, but she was too infirm to prevent it. Her feathers — already awry — fluffed with indignation. But within moments of being gathered against the lynx's belly fur she felt a plentiful warmth. She settled in and lay perfectly still. This warmth was what she needed more than anything else. She let the warmth of the lynx ease her pain, while the beating of its heart boomed through her, vibrating in her bones and soothing her wonderfully. It was the strangest dream she had ever had, but she let it comfort her, and wished only that it would not end any time soon.

* * *

Phoebe had woken up earlier in the night but could not get herself up. She was having another bad episode with her heart.

She'd been hearing noises over where the girl Nika lay — a suppressed cry, gasps, rustling sounds — by which she knew that the girl was still alive. She also knew the fire was nearly out, and that the girl needed warmth. She willed herself to get herself up to put some more logs on the fire. But for a long time, she could not move.

The slightest movement set her heart beating in a wild, stuttering way that would burst it apart if she did not heed its warning to stay perfectly still, until it was ready to beat properly again. *If* it would ever beat properly again . . .

This weakness had been her main worry when the Klurs brought Nika to her. In her present state she could barely take care of herself, let alone the badly injured girl. And yet, she had known as well as the Klurs did, that the girl would have a better chance with her than with the Tutners. So she had taken the girl in, hoping that she would have enough endurance to accomplish the task that her conscience led her to accept.

But now she could not revive the fire for the ailing girl.

71

She knew she was living on borrowed time. Whenever her heart stuttered she had to stop whatever she was doing, and concentrate on giving her heart its best chance to recover and continue beating for a while longer. Painfully and painstakingly, she had learned to nurse it along, cosseting it back into some semblance of a regular, life–extending rhythm.

Now she used every trick she had learned, to get herself out of her bed as soon as possible, and to get that fire going again for the girl.

When she finally eased herself out of bed, she was too weak and dizzy to stand upright, so she crawled to the hearth. It was too soon to tax her heart with this much effort, but she carefully pushed herself to her utmost.

At the hearth she put a small log onto the low dark embers, and tucked in some tinder — pieces of stick and bark, and one of the resin sticks that Ruth had brought. Her movements were clumsy and her breath, as she blew on the tinder, was ragged. But it lit, and a flame flared on the resin. She nursed the flame until the sticks and bark began to crackle and flame, sending small but healthy licks of fire around the curve of the log. Shaky from her efforts, she rested on her elbows, still kneeling into the hearth. She felt the first eddies of heat against her forehead and fingers, and concentrated on stilling her heart. Later, at the right time, she would add a larger log to the fire, and strive to build it up and this time, keep it going.

It was a while before she felt able to slide herself back and ease herself around on the floor, to look at the girl on the nearby pallet. When she did so, she could not make any sense of the patterns of light and dark in the flickering light. She searched for the shape of the coverlets that had been put over the girl: in the contrast between the coverlets and the darkness beyond it, she hoped to see the rise and fall of the girl's chest as she breathed — if she breathed.

Instead of a smooth plane of coverlets, what she saw looked more like . . . her old cat curled up on the dark hide, with the coverlets sprawled around it. But . . . that cat was long since dead. And what at first looked like her cat, was actually bigger than her cat had ever been.

The fire behind her burned brighter, and at the same time the patterns of light and dark shifted. There could be no mistake about it. A furry animal that *did* look like a very large cat *was* curled up on the hide. It had raised its head and was looking directly at her. Phoebe did not know where the girl Nika could have gone, but she could not see her anywhere in the room.

*   *   *

Tek raised his head and fixed his gaze on the old woman. With great deliberateness, he uttered the same low chuffing sound that he made when he first met her — when he admonished her for hurting him with her sharp stick. Now he was admonishing her again: she should have gotten the fire going much sooner. He had been able to keep the girl warm — shapeshifted as she was to owl, but unsheltered as he was, he was feeling the cold himself. The warmth of the fire was coming none too soon.

*   *   *

Phoebe recognized the lynx immediately by the odd sound that it made. Her heart, which had nearly settled down, jumped and stuttered with surprise and fear. And yet the lynx did not attack her, and the sound that it made — both the first time she had heard it and now — sounded so much like . . . a scold. And as before, there was something very human–like about this lynx. Then and now, the old, old stories of witches' familiars leapt to mind . . .

She feared the lynx, because she was weak and had no weapon close by — unless she could grab a stick or small log from the pile of fire wood at the hearth. Keeping her eyes fixed on the lynx, she groped to one side and behind, and grasped a stout stick from the pile of wood.

She brought it up in front of her, to use as a weapon if necessary. But the lynx just chuffed again, and this time its chuff sounded . . . disgusted. Then the bold creature got up, and stretched itself as if it feared nothing from her. It acted as if it was the most natural thing in the world for it to be ensconced in her home, chuffing its discontent at her.

It picked up a small fluffy ball of feathers in its mouth, and brought it to her lap. There at close range, it stared into her face, and

73

she could see the its face quite clearly in the firelight. The impression that she got was that the lynx was entrusting her with the object that it had brought to her, and it was warning her to be very careful with it.

The object in her lap moved and made small squawky sounds. Phoebe scooped it up very carefully in both hands, and tilted it so that she could see it better in the firelight. It was a very small owl, that seemed to be ill, or injured.

The lynx brought one of the coverlets over to Phoebe with its teeth. She used it to cover the owl as she held it against her breast.

How did this lynx and the owl get into her home? Where could the girl be? The front door was securely latched, and the shutters over the small high windows were all wedged shut. But Phoebe could now feel a light draft of cold air being drawn toward the fire from around the door to the cow's shed. With that much of a draft, the door could not be fully closed. Perhaps, she thought, the girl was not as badly injured as they had thought, and had somehow gotten herself out through the cow's shed. Or, possibly, she had collapsed in the shed . . .

Phoebe decided to check the shed. If the girl was in there, or had collapsed outside, she would need to be brought back in by the fire somehow.

With the lynx watching her every movement, Phoebe wrapped the little owl in the coverlet and left it on the hearth near the fire. She tried to stand up, but became too dizzy, and her heart beat too wildly. She crawled to the shed door on all fours.

She found, as she expected, that the door was open a crack.

Once inside the shed, she talked soothingly to the cow while she crawled around, searching for the girl. Then she crawled to the outer door, and was surprised to find that it was latched closed from the inside, just as she had left it. Clearly, the girl had not gone out that way. But she was not in the house, nor the shed . . .

From the strain of keeping her heart settled down, and the oddness of the lynx and the owl being in her home, Phoebe's mind was groggy and confused. She was worried about the girl and could not understand what had happened to her. But since the girl was not in her home, she had more immediate concerns.

In order to conserve her strength overall, she milked the cow before leaving the shed. With some warm milk in her and some rest by the fire, her heart might settle down enough for her to go outside at first light, and look around for the girl.

The cow tolerated Phoebe's crawling around; this was not the first time Phoebe had been too dizzy to stand in the cow's shed. After some soothing, the cow gave her milk and Phoebe took a draught of it.

Crawling out of the shed and toward the fire, she carefully pushed the bowl of milk along in front of her. She was nearly to the hearth before she glanced around for the lynx. It was sitting on its haunches, looking intently at the place where she had left the bundled–up owl.

To her amazement, the girl Nika was there, lying on her side! Even in the midst of her surprise, she was struck by how very thin the girl's bare body was — hardly more than skin and bones.

* * *

Nika had been watching Phoebe, taking in how haggard she was, and that she crawled instead of walked. She had shapeshifted back to being a girl shortly before Phoebe came back the cow's shed, and this time she knew she had not been dreaming.

Shapeshifting felt very strange to Nika, but at the same time it also felt completely natural. This was simply part of who she was. And the lynx, watching her change and purring at her, reassured her.

But the pain she was feeling as a girl was much greater than as an owl. Even with the warmth of the fire at her back, any effort to move set off a paroxysm of pain.

When Phoebe reached her and stared with obvious wonder and confusion, Nika told her, gasping, "I'm going to have to be . . . be owl for . . . for a while. Less . . . pain."

* * *

Phoebe's mind had already made the leap to connect the missing owl with Nika lying on the hearth, so actually watching Nika turn herself into an owl did not give her heart nearly as much trouble as it might have. When the transformation was finished Phoebe reached

75

out and with awe, gently stroked one of the owl's feathers with a fingertip.

Phoebe had led a simple life, leaving a barely civilized town in the east as a young bride, with little more than the hope of carving out a small farm somewhere in the inexhaustible western wilderness. She and her husband had achieved that much, wresting a homestead from the dense forest. Because of their ceaseless toil, a small stab of light penetrated the broad forestland, and warmed the cleared earth there enough to sustain them.

But within a few decades the years began to take more from her than they gave. She lost her husband and children to illnesses, accidents, and the worst of the indian raids.

Many women in her situation would have sold off the homestead and gone back east, or found accommodation in a city or town. But Phoebe had clung on, not questioning the harshness of her existence, and actually savoring as much of it as she could. She had lived on, barely above subsistence, but it was all she wanted or expected.

Throughout the years she had carefully observed the natural world, because survival required the fullest possible understanding. It might depend on knowing the difference between a freshet that would recede, and one that would grow to a roar and devastate all before it in its full flood. Or it might as easily depend on distinguishing the wild carrot that could heal, from the spotted water hemlock that would kill.

There was much she had learned, but there was much more that she would never understand. She would never understand why certain plants stayed green and healthy all winter, despite being covered with ice and snow. Or how some creatures came back to life in the spring. Though inexplicable, it was undeniably real, and this had taught her to trust her senses.

She was not going to doubt them now. She accepted that the girl Nika was a were–owl, and she wondered about the lynx as well . . . by its odd behavior and its very presence in her home, she wondered if this lynx might be another being that could, like Nika, change between person and animal.

She glanced over at the lynx. It was on all fours, sniffing the milk. It was a male, with the sinewy gauntness of considerable age. With an idle flash of intuition, Phoebe wondered if perhaps it might be too old to easily stay in its human form. Like Nika who felt less pain as an owl than as a person, perhaps the lynx had to remain as a lynx to avoid the debilitating infirmities of a human's advanced age.

Closer up, Phoebe could more clearly see the countless bare welts and gouges that marred its fur. From its scarred, ravaged face to a bald kink near the tip of its tail, there was no part of its body that had not been deeply lacerated or punctured. Phoebe marveled that any creature could sustain such terrible injuries and survive them.

* * *

Tek had seen the woman drink the white fluid several times before, and wondered what it tasted like. He lapped up some of it up, and then just a little more. It was not nearly as good as a mouse would have been, but there were no mice available at the moment.

* * *

Phoebe saw that the owl was staring at the bowl of milk. When the lynx left it, she slid it closer to the owl, and used a twig from the tinder pile to drip some of the milk into the owl's mouth. The owl swallowed some of it, but then closed its beak and its eyes, signaling that it had had enough. Its head bobbed with small spasms, and it drooped all over, looking ill, uncomfortable and groggy.

* * *

While Phoebe fed the milk to the owl, the lynx watched her every move with a distrustful glare. Then, since the fire was getting a little too hot, he picked the owl up gently in his mouth and moved it down from the hearth, onto the part of the hide pallet that was closest to the fire. The owl squawked and struggled weakly against being moved, but it had no choice but to submit.

On the pallet he nuzzled it, and curled himself carefully around it. What the girl needed now was warmth and rest, as he did. And he did not have to go outside to know that a huge snow pelt was already spreading over everything. This snow was going to be huge. He could feel its presence settling into his bones.

Even though he was now making himself very much at home in the old woman's living space, Tek did not try to hide his disdain for her.

But he would have to tolerate her for the time being. She seemed willing to help the girl, despite having failed to keep the fire up earlier. And she had accepted the girl as an owl, and seemed to care about keeping her warm now.

* * *

Phoebe put the coverlets around and over the lynx and owl, and built up the fire. The lynx seemed to know what the owl needed — warmth and rest for now. Warmth and rest . . . she could do with some of that herself. But there were a few things to do first.

Slowly she drank off some more of the milk. After a while she was able to get up and hobble into the cow's shed. She opened the shed's door to the outside. It was first light, but very dim because snow was coming down fast and thick. The cow went out into its fenced enclosure, while she pitched some fodder for it down from the loft. She did not have to muck out or fetch water for it, since Ruth had done that the evening before. She only had to break up the surface ice on the water.

The cow went out but it did not stay long in the ever–deepening snow.

Phoebe watched the heaviness of the snowfall with relief, since the Tutners were not likely to come for Nika during this much of a snow. And the driven flakes, obliterating everything beyond an arm's length, also gave her an idea, for thwarting the Tutners when they did come.

By the time she got back to the hearth she was exhausted. She dragged her chair closer to the pallet and sat for a while, wearily trying to think things through.

She expected to have considerable trouble with the Tutners when they came for the girl. Old Klur thought she could hold out against them, but he did not know them as well as she did. Her opinions, her preferences, meant nothing to them.

The Tutners, underneath their thin, superficial cordiality, were grasping and unprincipled. She had always managed to live in harmony with them, but only by never crossing them about anything serious.

She knew why they had isolated her from everyone but themselves, especially for the last several years. She had accepted it because she never expected to live this long, and it had not mattered to her, that they would have her property after her death.

But when the Klurs brought Nika to her yesterday, and worked with her to help her care for the girl, Phoebe realized that she had been paying too high a price for maintaining peace with the Tutners. The Klurs were decent, caring people who, she was sure, were *not* after her property, as the Tutners assumed they would be. Phoebe judged them to be truly good neighbors, and it rankled now that she had let the Tutners deprive her of their friendship.

She resolved that this would be no more. Even if she only had days to live, she was not going to let them limit her life any longer.

She still dreaded a confrontation with them when they came for the girl, but this snow storm gave her a useful buffer of time. That, coupled with the girl being a were–owl, gave her an idea for thwarting the Tutners. In her owl form the girl could be hidden, and the Tutners could be told, for instance, that she had dragged herself off in the night, before the big snow. They would search for her in the snow, perhaps, but they would never find her, as long as Phoebe could keep her hidden. Then, if the girl recovered, perhaps some indians passing through would take her with them, far from this valley and the Tutners.

Phoebe fully realized that she might not live long enough to see this plan through. But if she did not, then she felt certain that the Klurs would help the girl in her stead.

There were uncertainties, of course. Even with care, the girl might die, or be too maimed to leave the valley on her own. Or the Tutners might somehow discover what the girl was, and where she was hidden. But Phoebe resolved to help the girl as much as she could, and to never willingly return her to the Tutners.

Chapter 6
(The previous evening)

The Tutner household was in an uproar.

Sedric and Caleb had arrived on foot shortly after Sedric's father, Jacob, reached home from his arduous, unsettling trip to the port town across the river, where he had gone with three of his men to get essential supplies.

Jacob had not wanted to make the trip in the first place. It should not have been necessary, and he knew it would cost him dear.

It was all due to his wife and children's gross waste and mismanagement. Not only had they squandered the stores by their own profligacy, they had also failed to keep the thieving servants from raiding the storerooms.

On the day before the trip he had raged, shouting himself hoarse that if something like this had happened when *he* was a boy, everyone would have simply chewed on boiled leather until the spring growth rescued them from their want — those that managed to survive that long.

But his family knew that he was not going to let them starve. He would make the trip, and replenish their supplies in the town across the river. To hurry things along they went through the vocalizations and motions of contriteness and adulation. But it had been a long dreary winter; everyone was feeling sour and off. Thus their apologies rang hollow, and their affectionate phrasings had a tinny edge to them.

Their half-hearted efforts to mollify him were, in a way, more irritating than if they had made no effort at all. With his bile churning he cut short their blathering by gruffly announcing that he would go, but they had better be more careful with the stores in the future. When he set off on the trip early the next morning, he did not have to pretend to be in an exceedingly foul humor.

His mood worsened considerably when he reached the river town and did not get anything close to fair value for what he had brought with him to barter. Every single merchant took outrageous advantage of him. It was all sharp practice — all terse 'take or leave it'. There was not a single ignoramus, nor a soft touch, in the whole place, to enable him to cheat some of his own back. It was worse than a highway robbery! In the end, though, he had no choice but to accept their terms, or do without.

Then had come something that, if it meant what he thought it might, was much worse than all that preceded it.

On the ferry back over the river, the lowlife who was manning the boat's tow chains strolled up to him during a brief lull in his work, and addressed him with a shocking degree of familiarly, as if he had some claim on him. Jacob bristled and gave the river rat short shrift. But instead of backing away, and begging Jacob's pardon, the cheeky young man did something mystifying and unsettling. Slouching back to his cog work with a parting leer, the man sang his way through the raunchy old ditty about Saucy Polly.

Polly was a wanton tart who, as the song's chorus revealed with a lusty joy, always had a fine bouncing cross bun baking in her oven, which by the end of each chorus popped out bawling, 'Polly be me Ma, but jus' who, oh, who be my Pa?' Except that instead of the name 'Polly', in his rendition the ferryman garbled the tart's name into something like 'Catty', which Jacob came to feel was a name that was deliberately, uncomfortably close to his eldest daughter's name.

The man could not carry a tune, but he had the powerful lungs of a river man, and he sang with such bold abandon that his song rang out across the water, and echoed back with a disquieting warble.

Jacob was certain the man was mad, at first. He luxuriated in a thoroughly righteous outrage for himself and his family, until he happened to glance over at his own men. The three of them were exchanging looks and nodding their heads, all the while trying, without much success, to wipe knowing grins off their ugly mugs.

It was then that Jacob, in just a few moments, aged several years, as he contemplated the questions he would soon have to be asking his Carrie.

But surely not on this foul day, that was already going so miserably. Surely, delving into that swirl of doubt and dread could at least wait until the morrow.

When at long last Jacob reached home in the late afternoon, he wanted naught but to bask peacefully by his fireside. He planned to turn the supplies over to his wife and eldest son for disposal, after plucking out the two purchases that had cost him dearest — his new cask of brandy, and the pouch of Bradford's Best tobacco.

But he was going to be denied that small, earned pleasure, at least for some while yet. His son Sedric and the slave Caleb arrived home on foot shortly after he did, while he was still in the dooryard. He knew something was wrong, well before Sedric got close enough for him to see the abashed expression on his son's face. Sedric never bestirred himself to walk if he could ride. Clearly, the day had not yet delivered all of its ill tidings.

Jacob stood silent and stone–faced while his son Sedric told him about the logging accident. He already had a great weariness in both body and spirit, but he quickly separated the corn from the chaff in what he was hearing. The 'corn' of it was that his best mule was dead, along with one of his best servants, and a valuable logging sled had been smashed up, probably beyond repair. The 'chaff' was his son's labored explanation about how the dead servant was to blame for it all.

Jacob knew full well where the true blame for the accident lay — it was bound to have been fully the fault of his own bull–headed son. He could read it in Sedric's eyes, along with the boy's silent plea that he help him out of yet another tight spot that he had gotten himself into.

Jacob nodded his head slightly, signaling to his son that he could count on his father to back him, at least in front of all the world outside of the family circle. Privately between the two of them, of course, the boy would know that his father was not taken in by his story. Sedric had greatly disappointed him, yet again, and this time it was costing him a considerable chunk of property as well. It was a rather serious setback, but it would not break them. Family still came first. In future, though, the boy would have to do much better at following his counsel, than this.

Letting Sedric babble on about the depravity of the dead servant, he had just turned his thoughts to organizing some of the men to get her body off the hillside before nightfall, when he became aware that his daughter Carrie was screaming.

His wife Constance, his daughter Carrie and the younger children had all come out into the yard to greet him on his return, as was fitting. As was also fitting, they had stood by without interrupting their menfolk's serious talk.

But now Carrie was screaming her head off.

*   *   *

The moment Carrie saw her father's slight nod to Sedric, she knew that her cocky brother was going to get away with busting up the sled and killing the mule and servant. But *this* time he had gone too far because he had spoiled *her* plans too. He had collapsed that part of her castle in the air, where she got the mule and would no longer have to share the servant girl.

She descended into a screaming fury, and could not get out of it once she began. And she did not care a tot that there were menials all about who were hearing every word of it.

She was conscious of listening to herself screaming, as if it was someone else, and noticed with detachment that much of what she was screaming made no sense. But even an idiot would grasp the withering condemnation spewed at her brother and to some extent, in her father's direction as well.

The next thing that she was aware of, she was being shaken so hard that her teeth rattled. Somehow she had come to be inside the house, in a room with only the family present. All of them were looking at her, silent and wide eyed, except her father, who was the one shaking her.

He was yelling something. Well, he was bound to be angry about her having a fit in front of the servants and slaves. But she began to perceive that he was not yelling about her womanly pique. With a great effort she stilled her own violent need to emote so that she could understand what the damnation *he* was yelling about. He was saying . . . that he could see her condition, and that if something about it was true then she was cast off, and would never in her life be anything more than a lowly fishwife.

83

Soon after things quieted down in the house, Jacob left to retrieve the dead servant's body. He ordered Sedric to stay home, to punish him with idleness, when he would want to distract himself from his failings, by being active in the thick of things.

Jacob was determined to retrieve the body with appropriate promptness. It would not do to leave it out there on the hillside for wolves and vultures to feast on. They were always so remarkably quick to find fresh carrion.

He did not have to give his servants much, and he didn't. But they all knew they could count on him, when the time came, to see to it that they were buried properly. He was rather a stickler about it, for he knew it went a long way toward keeping them settled down.

This one's body would be tied in a sack and brought back to the homestead, where it would be banked under a mound of snow. When the ground thawed enough in the spring, it would be dug out of the snow and put into the servants' common grave.

*   *   *

Though the Tutner household had quieted down before Jacob left, there were currents running under its superficial calm.

*   *   *

Sedric had to work rather hard to keep from openly gloating. He yearned to make cutting remarks outside the door of his sister Carrie's room, loud enough for her to hear them. But Carrie might shout something nasty back, about the accident. He settled for clumping in his heavy boots past her door as often as possible.

He knew he was still in disgrace with his father because of the accident, and that many tedious hours lay ahead of him — hours of enduring his father's monotonous carping, about being more deliberate, and always taking due care. But the more immediate aftermath he had dreaded — that had been completely sidelined by the revelation of Carrie's incredible stupidity. What a fool she was, to have gotten herself pregnant by one of those half breeds that plagued the town's riverfront. After all her ridiculous 'great lady' airs, he so wanted her to know how much he was enjoying her fall from grace.

*   *   *

Carrie kept to her room. She had fully recovered from her fit, and was busily adjusting her plans. She was at least as adept as her father, at separating the corn in life, from chaff.

All that had *really* happened, after all, was that her father had found out, sooner than she had wanted him to, that she was expecting. As soon as he calmed down about it — perhaps as soon as the morrow — she would give him a fitting explanation. He was sure to see the advantages of staying with their long–held plan to set her up on Old Phoebe's homestead, with the husband she had lined up. She felt in no real danger of being cast off, or of having to be a fishwife.

She had completely overcome the strange sensations that had catapulted her into that unfortunate screaming fit. She hated to lose anything to Sedric, and she had so wanted to have that particular mule, and full charge of the servant girl Nika. But life was like that sometimes. In the calm after her storm, Nika's death meant nothing to her. Some nips from her cache of her father's brandy, hidden behind her closet wall, had helped her to see that, and had admirably settled her nerves.

As for Sedric — he could clomp back and forth outside her door as often and as loudly as he wished. He could wear the floor boards out, for all she cared. She would be out on her own before long, while he, with his unstoppable idiocy, was bound to bring ruin to everything he bent his efforts to. It was as inevitable as the seasons of the year.

She got a little bored, so she amused herself by practicing her mimicry. In the privacy of her own room she mimicked *all* of her family's voices.

*   *   *

Jacob's wife Constance kept herself busy with own children, occupying them well out of the way of their much older step brother and sister. She was not a particularly imaginative woman, but for a short while, in the midst of Sedric's lame excusing and Carrie's hysterics, she glimpsed that there might be a brighter future ahead for her own children, if she could somehow turn her husband against his two eldest offspring. It had never seemed remotely possible before. But now, as she sent her own children to bed early, she envisioned a few ways to widen the gap between her husband and those two uppity, insufferable step children of hers.

* * *

Gradually, all three of them — Sedric, Carrie and Constance — began to wonder what could be delaying Jacob's return.

But only after he had been gone at least twice as long as they expected, did the barking of the dogs announce his return.

Sedric and Constance went out to greet him in the dooryard, hoping to gauge his mood.

He was grim, but silent. And they could see for themselves that he had not brought the servant's body back with him.

He gave them dark looks and made no answer to their questioning gazes, except to say gruffly, "Morrow."

Sedric tried to find out what had happened from the men who had gone out with him. But they informed him that they'd been ordered to say nothing. Like it or not, he and Constance would have to await the morrow, to find out what had happened.

Jacob at long last sat before his fire alone, sipping from his new keg of brandy and drawing on fresh tobacco in his pipe. His wife had left him there and gone to bed, when he ignored all her quiet, hesitant questions after his comfort. He also paid no attention to his son Sedric's diffident good night wish, before the oaf clumped off to his own bed.

Carrie observed him from the door of her room, and was smart enough to leave him completely to himself. The morrow would be soon enough to straighten him out, and rein him in.

* * *

The house settled into its nighttime quiet.

Jacob had deliberately kept them from knowing that the little servant girl might still be alive, and that the Klurs had taken her to Phoebe's for care. He would inform them on the morrow. In the meantime, let them stew. He wanted to sort through his thoughts, before his family added whatever cacophony they might to the situation.

He had taken two men with him in one of the light sleighs. Caleb was necessarily one of the two: he could take them directly to where the girl's body lay.

At the bottom of the hill, they unhitched the mule to take it up with them, without the sleigh.

Trudging up the hill in the fading light, they saw that there were a lot more foot and hoof prints in the snow than there should have been — more than would account for the logging sled's one–way trip up the hill, and Sedric and Caleb coming off the hill on foot. Caleb's comment on it was to remind Jacob that he and Sedric had met the Klurs on their way home, not too far from the bottom of the hill, and that Sedric had told them about the accident.

It nettled Jacob that the Klurs had apparently gone up the hill and made free to satisfy their idle curiosity about the accident. He had never liked them, but had not thought them so low as to go up there to gape and gloat over his family's misfortune.

When they reached the place of the accident, it angered him when he found that the Klurs had taken the girl's body away with them. Clearly, they did not think that he knew his duties as a master. Their interference was insufferable, uncalled for, and an affront to his superior standing in the valley.

He took a quick look around before they went back down. Already a vulture was at the dead mule. It flew off when they approached, but it was sure to be back with some others as soon as they left. He gave a cursory look at the smashed sled, and at the number of logs scattered all about. Then he hurried the mule and his two men back down the hill, and directed the sleigh toward the Klurs' homestead.

Long before he reached it, the Klurs' mongrels started their loud and furious barking, alerting their masters that someone was approaching their wretched domain.

Annoyingly, the raucous barking went on long after they arrived. Klur was insultingly slow at coming out and quieting them down.

When Klur finally sauntered up to his gate, where Jacob waited for him in his sleigh, he did not invite Jacob to come inside, which set a very unfriendly tone. He was accompanied by his two daughters — the older, old maidy one, and the younger one that was not nearly

as homely, and might yet catch herself a man if she was lucky —
someone who would be content to eventually take over this gritty
little farm from Old Klur, when he passed on.

The sky had darkened and Jacob could not see the two women's
faces very well, but he could feel them staring at him. It threw him
off a little. The way they silently flanked their father had an odd,
formal look to it, almost as if they were high priestesses in attendance
at some ancient, ungodly ritual.

This fanciful image harkened back to when Jacob, as a boy, had
been fortunate enough to receive nearly a full year of classical
education. At the time it was quite unusual for these parts.

The opportunity had arisen when a defrocked minister of a high
church in a city along the Atlantic came hastily west. In order to have
a livelihood he set himself up as a schoolmaster in the port town,
advertising Greek and Latin lessons in addition to pedagogical
rudiments. Jacob's father wanted one of his sons to acquire this
refinement, that he himself lacked. Jacob was about the right age for
it, and could be spared for a while on the farm, so he was sent to the
town for a trial year of fancy schooling, where he worked nights in
his uncle's tavern for his board, and by day attended classes with
boys from some of the town's wealthier families.

Jacob never did learn much Latin, nor any Greek, but it was not
because the erstwhile minister had graduated near the bottom of his
divinity school class. It was because the man, as a newly minted
schoolmaster, quickly despaired of getting anything lodged in the
heads of his loutish students, that even vaguely resembled either the
Greek alphabet or a Latin verb conjugation.

To preserve his livelihood, he had to keep up the appearances of
teaching them something. And to curtail their incessant and riotous
brawling in his classroom, he had to find a way to hold their
attention. He set them to rote copying classical ciphers onto their
slates and, when they had had about as much of that as he could
reasonably expect, he rewarded their penmanship exercises by
amusing them to the best of his ability, with exciting stories about the
lives of the ancient Greeks and Romans.

Fortunately for everyone concerned, he was a rather gifted
storyteller. Ever afterward, Jacob's life was immeasurably enriched by

his having heard so many intriguing tales of blood–soaked rituals, horrific hand–to–hand combat and bizarre, half–human mythological creatures.

The most enthralling of the stories were about the ancient world's harsh, judgmental women. Always in these stories the schoolmaster's voice shook with a deeply felt passion, which never failed to draw the boys into a spellbound silence, for these were the stories that always ended horrifically for the hapless young men and boys of the ancient world.

Whenever disaster struck in Jacob's own life, the schoolmaster's vivid stories about the three cruel hags of fate would come to his mind. The uncertainties and odd twists of his own life had so often given credence to the tales of the workings of those ugly sisters, who cackled with particular glee as they snipped the life thread of an innocent young man, and callously tossed it onto a close–by dunghill. As recently as earlier today, looking out over the river to calm himself, after enduring the indignities of the ferryman's suggestive and ill–sung song about Saucy Polly, Jacob had derived some solace from imagining that those three old crones just might, at that very moment, be doing their secret, fatal dance close in around that very ferryman. For the man's job was one of the most dangerous on the riverfront: in an instant of distraction a body part might be — and often was — caught between the towing chains and the cogs, and crushed there to a bloody pulp. And with some frequency the maimed men died of their injuries a short time afterward. Leaning on the boat's railing, Jacob had heartily wished that the three ugly sisters would soon deliver this fate to the insolent man.

Later at the Klurs' gate, Jacob was oddly but strongly reminded of another of the schoolmaster's stories — one that came to his mind much less frequently than the stories about the fates. It was the story of the priestesses who in ancient times stood beside an altar where infant boys were sacrificed, and caught their dripping blood in wide bowls of shining, beaten copper.

Jacob did not know why the two stone–faced Klur sisters, standing slightly behind their father on either side of him, brought those ancient priestesses so much to mind. But the juxtaposition unsettled him. He had intended to be peeved and demanding with

Klur, perhaps even openly rude. But faced with Klur's cold silence, and the gazes of the two shadowy women, he began instead with a truculent question.

"Well then, Klur. Were you thinking I'd risk leaving the girl's body out on the hill this night?"

"Why, no, Jacob," came Klur's slow, measured reply.

"Then why did you take her body?"

"Truly, Jacob, my Ruth and I found no body."

Klur was deliberately talking in riddles, which greatly irritated Jacob. But it also spooked him, because the ancients in their rituals also spoke their oracles in riddles. The fanciful impression strengthened, that Klur was flanked by dangerous priestesses.

"What?! No body?!" he asked, a little less righteously that he had intended.

"Aye. None. For to the best that I be knowing, Jacob, the girl yet lives. Though surely, only barely now. We found her hurt terrible bad, and senseless."

"Ah! I fathom you. You found her alive and brought her here, for me to take on back with me. Uncommonly neighborly of you. We'll just —"

"Nay, Jacob."

More damnation riddles! But the aura of priestesses and ancient rituals had been fading with every commonplace word uttered by Klur.

"Nay? What mean you, Klur?" Jacob spoke sharply.

"I mean just what I say. I mean nay."

*   *   *

Klur, carefully watching his seething neighbor, chose not to elaborate right away. He knew full well that his drawn out word play was nettling Jacob. He was doing it on purpose, to unsettle him. The more he could unsettle Jacob, the better.

When he and Ruth had taken the girl to Phoebe, his earlier inclination to help the girl had strengthened with everything he did to get her settled there. The inclination hardened into a moral duty that he felt, to do his utmost to help her, with what little he had.

Now, facing the girl's angry master, he gauged that the more he was able to unsettle him, the better were the injured girl's chances.

Whatever he said now was not likely to hold much sway with Jacob, but he was determined give it his best try.

The two men regarded each other coldly, until Klur leaned in toward Jacob. "We found her hurt terrible bad," he repeated with slow, deliberate emphasis. His voice, which had been soft and neutral before, took on an accusatory timbre. "Hurt in an accident that no *prudent* man, such like yourself, Jacob, would *ever* let happen. Her head be broken, and like as not her neck, which be strangely twisted. The dark center of one eye, be much larger than that of the other. A leg broken for certain. Probably an arm as well. She lies floppy, still. She wakes not. Her life hangs by a thread, Jacob — a thin thread. And t'was *your boy Sedric* what caused this."

Jacob started some bluster, but Klur leaned in closer and cut him short with, "We *both* be knowing that, Jacob."

Jacob reared back from his neighbor and regarded him with an ill–concealed anger of his own. "What is it that you want, Klur?" he barked.

Now was the time to shoot the bolt. "Phoebe's place was closest, so we took her there. Move her no further, Jacob, 'til she be well, or she be dead. Else you want the blame on *you* as well this time, alongside your son."

"Blame?! What blame?! She be my *property*, Klur."

"Her *life* be your responsibility, Jacob."

"*You've* no rights in this! And I will judge for myself what's best for my servants!"

"Aye. You be the best judge, for you bear the full responsibility," Klur shot back.

"It was an accident," Jacob spluttered, "and there be no case against me, for she has no standing. The girl's an *indian*, and besides she has no kin."

"I do not speak of law courts. I speak of an accident caused by your son, that should never have been. And *now* it depends on you, Jacob, whether we here feel a need to speak out on it."

* * *

Jacob was keen to question his interfering neighbor about what he meant by that, but he was increasingly conscious that the two men with him were hearing every word. One a slave, and the other

91

indentured. Neither of them should be hearing any more of this kind of talk by an interfering freeman. It might well stir them the wrong way.

"I'll trouble you no further, Klur, since you do not have the girl here," he said brusquely, to which Klur made no response.

Just before they left, the older Klur daughter stepped forward and quietly called Jacob's slave Caleb to the gate. She had his jacket in her hands. She handed it over the gate to him, telling him that they had found it on the hillside, and that she thought he might be needing it now that the thaw was ending. Caleb took it from her with a mumbled thanks, and put it on right away, over the one he had borrowed for this trip. A harsh wind had sprung up, and the air sweeping in was indeed much colder.

Despite the long day that had already held far too much misery for him, Jacob intended to go direct to Phoebe's hovel from the Klur's. At the very least, he wanted to assess the girl's condition for himself.

But as he turned the sleigh around and headed away from Klur's dreary place, his neck got hot with the feeling that the older Klur daughter was still standing by the gate, staring fixedly at him. It was a ridiculous notion, but Klur's talk and the two women's stares had unsettled him more than he wanted to admit.

And . . . full dark had come on, under low clouds that were blowing in.

And . . . it had been a very long while since the last time he had gone to Phoebe's hovel. He was not really sure whether he could find the path to it in the dark, without a lot of floundering around.

And . . . if he did find the path, it would probably be too narrow for this sleigh, which meant a long walk in from the road and back out.

So he changed his mind. All in all, it would be better to wait until the morrow to go to Phoebe's place. Then, more rested and in the light of day, he would be better able to assess the girl's condition, and the overall situation.

When he reached the main road he turned the sleigh toward the direct route home, instead of the direction that would take him by the path to Phoebe's place.

*   *   *

Klur's daughter Ruth had in fact been staring fixedly at Jacob's back as he left. She listened as well. When she heard the Tutners' sleigh turn in the direction of his homestead, she let her father know that they would have enough time to take the supplies to Phoebe, that they had been gathering when Jacob arrived. Jacob might yet go to Phoebe's later in the night, but for the time being he was returning home.

*   *   *

Later at his fireside with his third brandy nipperkin for the night, Jacob thought that Klur was probably bluffing about disparaging him and his son, if he took the girl home with him on the morrow, and she ended up dying from her injuries at his homestead. But . . . if he wasn't bluffing, and the girl did die in his attic . . . wagging tongues, especially if they did most of their flapping behind his back . . . at best they were like pesky itches that one could never quite get at to scratch. But at worst . . . sometimes gossip did a surprising amount of harm. With a shiver, his thoughts returned to the three ancient sisters of fate — Chloe, Leonora and Agatha, if he recollected the schoolmaster's stories rightly. The most fearsome of the three was Agatha. She was the one who at times went berserk and hacked with wild abandon at the life threads of innocent men.

Jacob slipped into a brandy–addled dose, in which this Agatha of past imaginings became Klur's older daughter. She carried a whip made from her long, sharp–edged tongue, which she used to drive him from his home, out into a cold night. Jacob woke with a start at the crack of the whip, which proved to be nothing more than a log in the fire, split open by the heat.

*   *   *

The wind groaned off and on through the night. When the Tutner household woke at first light the next morning, immediate needs overruled all other plans and intentions. There was nearly three feet of snow on the ground, and snow was still falling heavily. Necessarily, Jacob's trip to Phoebe's would have to be postponed for a few days.

Nearly all of the help in the Tutner household worked to clear paths between the house, barns and sheds. All of the morning's chores took much longer than usual. Everyone breakfasted late.

After breakfasting, Jacob informed his family in a brusque 'by the way', that the servant Nika had survived the accident, but was badly injured and was being cared for by Old Phoebe, for the time being. He then told Carrie that he wanted to meet with her in private.

By then he was amenable to accepting her assurances that the yodeling river rat was certainly *not* the father of his grandchild–to–be, and that she had in fact snubbed his highly improper advances with laudable persistence. In fact, she had repulsed the man with so much verve — according to *her* version of events — that, in order to spite her, the dirty louse made his crude and false insinuations against her.

Jacob's relief was palpable, and almost comical to Carrie, as she smugly stated that the actual father–to–be was the son of a prosperous farmer in the next valley over, and that he was agreeable to the marriage — provided of course that Carrie brought their old relative's homestead with her into it.

Carrie paused delicately at this point.

Within moments, her father was questioning her minutely about the state of Old Phoebe's health when she visited her the previous morning. He was greatly encouraged by her report that Phoebe's demise was imminent.

He and his daughter slipped back into their old comfortable groove. By the time he gave her leave to go and help her stepmother, he was thinking about how fortunate it was that his trip to Old Phoebe's hovel would now be delayed a few days more, because of the heavy snowfall. In the interim, caring for the injured servant would drain his old relative's remaining strength, and perhaps also her meager stores of food. If the girl recovered, she would be of no use to him — and a considerable burden for a great long time — much too long. In his mind, he had already written her off. With any luck, he mused, when he did get to Phoebe's hovel after all this snow — in a few days' time at the earliest, he would find both his old relative and the broken–up servant stone cold dead. First the old woman would succumb to a failed heart, in all likelihood, and then the girl would die from her injuries and exposure after the old woman died. Better yet, the heavy snow might collapse the hut's roof. Then the woman and girl would be dead when he got there, *and* he would be spared some of the work of tearing down the hut . . .

But he did not devote much more thought to the extraneous old woman and servant girl. His busy mind turned to plans for clearing the brushy fields of Old Phoebe's property, and for building a fine new house and barn on the property for his daughter and new son–in–law.

After her meeting with her father, Carrie did *not* go to help her stepmother, as he had bade her. She went instead to her room, for some more quiet reflection and relaxation. All was going along rather well again. It made no difference to her *now*, that the servant girl Nika was apparently alive, and might eventually recover from her injuries. Like her father, she wrote the girl off. She picked another female servant to be the one that she would take with her to her new homestead.

* * *

Throughout the area the snow fell heavily all day. By the time it stopped near nightfall, it was without doubt one of the biggest snowstorms in the collective memory — about seven feet altogether, though by the end of the next day it would settle to a denser four or five feet. Anyone wanting to get out and about in it would have to use indian snowshoes, but nearly everyone was prepared to wait for the snow to settle. Then, with logs hitched to ox teams, the snow would be packed down on the main roads and the spurs to the homesteads, for sleighs and sleds to run on them. If the temperature moderated and melted some of the snow, and if no more snow fell in the interim, then everyone would be able to travel fairly easily on most of the main roads, in three or four days' time.

95

Chapter 7

'If wishes were horses then beggars would ride' . . .

Contrary to Jacob's wishful notion, the roof on Phoebe's home did *not* collapse under the weight of snow. The building had started out as a mere shed, but it was well built, and withstood the heavy snowload weighing down its creaking old bones.

In all, four full days passed before Jacob and his son Sedric made their way through the snow to Old Phoebe's hut.

More than not, those were days of peace and wonderment for Phoebe, Nika and Tek, cached as they were with adequate stores, and insulated, for the most part, from the rest of the world.

The first day started out very quietly. All three of them slept or at least rested until early afternoon. Nika slept and dozed fitfully because, even as an owl, it was too painful for her to do otherwise. Phoebe fashioned a small splint for Nika's injured owl leg, with a loop in the binding for Nika to pull it loose, if she needed to change back into a girl. The splint helped a little, but pain kept her very still.

Phoebe slept as much and as well as she could, to conserve her heart's strength.

Tek only rested, for the most part. As a lynx he was primarily a night creature and normally slept during the day, but he felt exposed out in the open, in the old woman's living space. If it wasn't for the girl, he would be snug in the loft over the cow, sleeping through the snowbound day.

He was the most wakeful and alert of the three. He had been dozing off and on, spending his awake time thinking about the injured girl, whom he approved of, and was growing fond of. He felt a connection with her because he now knew not only that she was one of the People, like himself, but that she was an owl shapeshifter like his beloved Tsihi had been. He also liked everything he observed

96

about her character. And she was wisely staying in her owl shape, to hasten her physical recovery.

He mulled over how he had come to be here, and how the girl was now here and clearly in need of his care and help. He wondered whether the great bear spirit had led him to come here. He could not be certain about it, but unless the bear spirit gave him a clear sign to the contrary, her wellbeing was going to be his paramount concern.

He ignored the old woman as much as possible. The incident when she poked him with her sharp stick had happened over two moons ago, but he did not think he would ever forgive her for it. More immediately, he did not approve of the way she had endangered the girl, by letting the fire burn down the preceding night.

And she was *not* of the People. She did not have anything like their scent, nor anything like their nature. It was unnatural for a woman to live alone, and yet she apparently had been living that way for a very long time. And she drank the mother's milk of that great, lumbering bess. To Tek, this was both unnatural, and it took untoward advantage of the beast. And she couldn't be very intelligent, because she did not take proper care of herself, when the means to do so was practically within reach of her fingertips.

The previous night when he had examined her living space, it perplexed him when he found some o–se hanging on her wall, tied up in a dry, dusty bunch with other plants that had no healing value whatsoever. Why, he wondered, did she endure so much heart suffering when she had gathered a cure for it and had it ready to hand? Of course, with someone as far gone as she was, one had to be very careful with the dosage. Perhaps she was afraid that she would take the wrong amount, and thereby do herself in . . .

For a while Tek easily pushed aside the notion that he should try to help her. When he disliked someone, he could be very firm.

But eventually he had to admit to himself that he had better try. Clearly, she was necessary to the girl's wellbeing, essential for doing a myriad of things — like keeping the fire going, which was something he could not do. Thus far she had done that poorly, but a fire that was re–started late, was better than no fire at all.

If the old woman suddenly keeled over dead, he could not take care of the girl by himself, in her fragile condition.

* * *

Nika managed to sleep through most of the afternoon. Little noises of the lynx and Phoebe moving around did not disturb her enough to waken her. As the light was fading though, she began to be groggily aware that sleep had done her some good. Her head, neck and right leg still hurt terribly, but the pains in the rest of her body had eased somewhat.

She became aware that Phoebe was speaking to her.

"Nika, can you be hearing me? Can you understand?"

Nika opened her owl eyes. Phoebe was looming over her, looking worse than ever. Her breath was shallow, and her skin was pasty grey. She also looked worried. The lynx was close by, staring down at her. Nika thought mussily that it looked worried too.

"Nika, if you can understand what I am saying, can you give me a sign of it? Can you, perhaps, be opening your beak, or bobbing your head for me?

Nika opened her beak, and uttered an "Awk!"

"Ah, I be thinking you give me answer."

Nika opened her beak wide again and provided another "Awk!"

Phoebe nodded at this confirmation. "This so relieves me, Nika, for I have an important question." She moved a battered pewter cup to where Nika could see it, and tipped it so that Nika could see that it held a slimy brown liquid, with bits of vegetative sludge floating in it. "I would like to know," she asked humbly, "if you think that I should drink this?"

* * *

Phoebe then explained — slowly, in case it was difficult for Nika to understand her — that the lynx had been acting very strange all afternoon. It had roused her from a doze, and then, when it could see that she was watching it, it stood at the south wall where all of her herbs were hung. Several times it looked up at the herbs, and then back at her, but when she did nothing but gaze at it without comprehension, it emitted one of its odd little chuffs and leapt up repeatedly until it succeeded in knocking most of the tied bunches and bundles of herbs off their pegs. It then seemed to take delight in tossing some of them around and crushing them. But it was very careful with others, and with one bunch in particular. It picked that one up gingerly in its teeth and brought it over to her.

This would have made some sense to her if the lynx had brought her some of the yarrow, or the chamomile. Then she would have understood that the lynx wanted her to prepare something for Nika — a fresh brew of fever tea, perhaps, or a salve for muscle aches.

But instead, it brought her a tied bunch of plants that contained no herbs at all. It was just some vegetation that she had gathered, bound together and hung to dry out, simply because each plant had some combination of stalk, leaf, flower or seed pod that pleased her. Every fall she made at least one such arrangement, for no other purpose than to be interesting shapes and textures to look at, on dreary winter days.

Phoebe asked the lynx if it could understand her words, but the lynx looked back at her with a blank expression. It then batted impatiently at the flax twine she had used to bind the plants together. She loosened the binding, and spread the plants out on the floor beside her.

The lynx pawed at one plant in particular — a gangly–leaved one with a stiff stalk and — when fresh — a milky sap. Phoebe knew no name for it; she just called it bane because it looked similar to dogsbane.

She caught on that the lynx wanted her to separate that one from the rest. It then led her through a series of steps, which culminated in a murky, vile–smelling brew bubbling in a very small pot over the fire. At each step she had to guess at what the lynx wanted her to do. When she guessed right, it let her proceed. When wrong, it stopped her with a paw set firmly on the back of her hand — sometimes set there hastily with its claws unsheathed enough to prick her skin, and she had to guess again at what it wanted her to do.

It was a long, arduous process. Besides it being hard to understand what the lynx wanted, the lynx was extremely finicky about which parts of the plant could go into the pot. The thinner, smaller stems could go in, but not the tougher stems or any of the fibrous stalk. Conversely, the larger leaves could go in, but not the smaller ones. And the lynx nearly bit her when she moved to drop some of the plant's dried flower pods into the pot — it snapped at her savagely and growled a fierce menace. It frightened her a few other times as well, by its intense stares, its low muttering growls and, occasionally, its agitated pacing in a tight loop.

The lynx always seemed to have a sour expression, which the crisscrossing scars accentuated. It also had mannerisms that struck her as being impatient or dismissive — not unlike what a crotchety old man might do, who was very set in his ways, and could not bring himself to approve of her.

Strange as it was to be taking instruction from a lynx, Phoebe cooperated to the best of her ability. She assumed that the brew was for Nika — something that the lynx thought the girl would need to get well. She had seen how affectionate and protective the lynx was toward Nika. Surely the brew was for the girl, and the lynx wanted it to be just right for her sake.

Phoebe also supposed that the brew was something that would be cooled and applied to the girl's bruised skin in a poultice, or mixed with some lard to use as a salve. She judged that it was much too harsh a brew to drink, and besides, it smelt too much of steeped lilac, which she knew was safe when applied externally, but was poisonous to ingest.

She was quite surprised when, after some further trial and error to determine what the lynx wanted her to do, she realized that the brew was intended for her, and that the lynx wanted her to drink it, and was in fact quite impatient for her to drink it.

She balked then, not so much because the lynx obviously disliked her, but more because the expression on its face seemed to have hardened into something harsher, more calculating and . . . strangely avid. She also thought there was an implacable savagery in its eyes, which had not been there before. It was as if the lynx was looking forward to watching her reaction to drinking the brew, in a way that would definitely not end well for her.

Phoebe had survived thus far in life by trusting her instincts, and deep down, she now felt that she should not trust the lynx. She shook her head slowly and firmly, signaling to the lynx that she would not drink the brew.

She rather expected the lynx to become agitated and more insistent, but instead it went very still, and Phoebe thought that she could trace a sudden expression of intense sadness in its eyes, which made her doubt her instincts somewhat. But . . . not enough for her to change her mind.

It was then that she had glanced over to see how Nika was doing. Nika as owl was stirring a little, so Phoebe thought of asking her. Perhaps Nika would know whether it was safe to drink the brew.

* * *

Phoebe had in fact misinterpreted the expression on Tek's face, as he had tried to get her to drink some of the brew. What she thought was harsh and calculating, was actually an intense watchfulness, to make sure that she drank enough of the brew, but not too much. Too little would do no good; while too much could be rapidly and irreversibly fatal.

And what Phoebe had thought was an implacable savagery shining in his eyes, was actually his desperate uncertainty — had he gauged her size and condition, and the brew's strength, accurately enough to avert her immediate demise? He had grown up watching the shamans and medicine women of his People making and administering this heart brew. He had often heard their serious talk droning on and on about how much was enough, and how much would be fatal. But he had never made it or administered it himself, and did not want to accidentally kill the old woman.

But then it was all for naught, because she refused to drink it.

What Phoebe then saw in Tek's eyes, she *did* correctly interpret as a sudden, crushing sadness. Tek knew that without the brew, she would not survive much more than another day. For the sake of the ailing girl, that greatly saddened him. Without the old woman's help in tending her, the girl was very likely to die as well.

But that sadness was deepened by his realization, that it was due to his own mistakes that the old woman refused to drink his brew. He had completely misjudged her.

Too late he saw that he had squandered her trust, and that her trust was essential. It was by his own fault that first the woman, and then the girl, were going to die. He had not only let down the girl, but also perhaps the bear spirit, if it had sent him here to aid her.

101

He had assumed all along that the old woman was ruled by selfishness — he thought he had seen it in her living alone, in her taking the milk from the bess, and especially in her acceptance of the girl into her home, which he had assumed was to gain the generous supplies brought in with her, of food and other essentials.

He had been getting some inkling of a different, better person by the careful and patient way she persevered with the making the brew, but he had not really understood her until it was too late. For it was only at the end, when she registered such complete surprise that the brew was for her, that he saw his error, and read her mistrust of him in her eyes. Then it was too late, much too late, to turn such a one as he now understood her to be, from her refusal.

But then the old woman turned to the girl in her owl shape and, from the tone of her voice, asked some questions, and then talked to her.

And talked.

And talked.

And talked.

For such a great long time.

It was the most words that Tek had yet heard the woman speak.

He could understand none of them, but the tone and modulation of her voice reassured him. The voice was calm and measured, quietly confident and reasonable, if a little perplexed at times. The old woman was explaining something to the girl, and he thought it was about him, and the brew. A spark of hope lit in his breast. He sat quietly on his haunches, watching them both.

Occasionally the woman glanced his way while she was talking. After the first time, Tek cocked his head to one side and tried to look back at her winningly. His pride took a blow, but that was not important now. It was his own mistakes that had brought him to this critical juncture with her.

At length the woman finished with her explaining, and, by the inflection of her voice at the end, Tek could tell that she asked the owl a question.

* * *

The owl turned its head, and starred at him with its huge dark eyes — oh, so much like Tsihi. Then it shaped itself back into a girl and, clearly, into a much more painful state. Both Tek and Phoebe could see that her neck was causing her the most trouble now. She had been able to turn it slowly when she was an owl, but as a girl she could not move it at all. It looked like it was not properly aligned.

Nika shuddered, and then tried to suppress the agony that the shudder caused.

Phoebe had told her of the brew making, and of what the lynx wanted her to do with it. She had told her as well that she thought that the lynx might be a were creature like Nika was, but that it did not seem to be able to change into being a person as easily as Nika could. And Phoebe had also told her that she did not think that the lynx could understand Phoebe's words.

Nika asked the lynx, in her native language, whether it could understand her. Borrowing Phoebe's method, she asked the lynx to bob its head for 'yes', if it understood her.

After starring back at Nika with a perplexed but eager expression on its face, the lynx very deliberately stood up, turned itself around, and sat back down.

Nika told Phoebe that she thought the lynx had some understanding of her words . . . but that there were apparently some differences as well.

She enlisted Phoebe's help and used the simplest phrases when speaking to the lynx. First, she had Phoebe nod her head, and then she asked the lynx to copy that gesture, and to use it to mean 'yes'. In the same way, she established that when the lynx shook its head from side to side, that would mean 'no'. Tek then contributed his own signal, for when he needed her to ask her question again but in different way: he tilted his head and chuffed softly whenever what she was asking did not make any sense to him.

Nika tired very quickly. Her pain increased relentlessly. But she stuck with questioning the lynx, until she was at last able to tell Phoebe that she thought that she should drink the brew, but should do so cautiously, always following the lynx's guidance as closely as possible.

There had come a point in the questioning, when Nika asked the lynx if Phoebe needed to drink the brew in order to continue living. Knowing the significance of Phoebe's fading, gasping breaths, and not mistrusting the lynx as much as Phoebe had, the question seemed to Nika to be a logical one, and an important one to ask. The lynx understood her, and emphatically nodded 'yes'.

Nika's pain was reaching an unbearable level. With her voice dropping to a whisper, she excused herself to Phoebe in her language, and to the lynx in some approximation of his. She turned herself back into an owl. The lynx nuzzled her tenderly, and Phoebe tucked the coverlet around her gently.

* * *

Phoebe then picked up the cup, and indicated to the lynx that she was ready to drink the brew. There was fear in her eyes, but also . . . trust.

When she took a tiny sip of the brew, she nearly gagged on its revolting smell and taste, and the slimy consistency. But she continued to sip it until the lynx bade her pause by a firm paw on her arm. By then her stomach was churning rebelliously, and she felt so dizzy that she keeled over beside the hearth.

The next hour or so was a blur to Phoebe. Her heart slammed in her chest, her head felt strangely loose and floating, and her stomach jolted as if poked with sharp needles. She wanted only to curl up and breathe as shallowly as possible, until the worst passed. But the lynx kept prodding her to raise her head and look at him. After a while she realized that he was checking on how she was doing. She tried to get her head up enough to suit him each time, though it felt as wobbly as a flail.

Once he prodded and snarled at her until she got herself up enough to sip some more of the brew. Her hands shook so much that she nearly dropped the cup. The lynx made her lower the cup to the hearth, and sprawl herself down low enough to sip from the tilted cup, to lessen the risk of spilling its contents.

Phoebe lay back down, broke out in a sweat, and then felt freezing cold despite the fire. Her body convulsed with shaking. At that point the lynx dragged her quilt over from her bed with his teeth, and draped it over her. He then lay on top of the quilt, a firm weight of bone, flesh and fur balanced on top of her shuddering, quivering body.

She felt about to vomit but with the lynx perched on top of her she could not raise herself up to spew whatever her stomach sent up. The best she could do was tip her mouth downward so that if she did puke, she would be less likely to choke on whatever phlegm or slurry came up. But she never did vomit. Instead she fell into a queasy daze.

At length she slipped from the daze into a deep, sound sleep.

She did not know how long she slept but when she woke, she felt more refreshed than she had in a great many months — in years even. Her blood hummed sweetly throughout her body, nourishing it like an elixir from scalp to toes. She had forgotten that she had ever felt this good. She felt . . . something like youth. It was marvelous, amazing!

The cow was lowing in her shed. It must be past the time for the evening milking. Phoebe opened her eyes, and found the lynx's face inches away. It was examining her eyes and the skin of her face minutely.

Whatever the lynx saw apparently satisfied it, because it backed away, and left her to do whatever she wished. She was relieved that, for the time being, the lynx did not want her to drink any more of the brew. She realized that the brew, as administered by the lynx, had saved her life. But she also understood, from its violent effects on her body, that not much would separate an effective dose of it, from a fatal one.

She sat up, and then rose up fully, a new woman. She was not the least bit dizzy. She felt so good — able to do so many things she had not been able to do in a very long time. She was sure she could pick up a full bucket of water, instead of having to scoot it along the floor. She could fling her bedding off her bed if she wanted to, and beat it soundly to air it. Why, she could even cut and split some wood!

She checked on Nika, who was snoozing about as comfortably as could be expected.

She noticed the backs of her hands when she picked up her milking bowl. They were no longer withery grey; they looked pinker, and her skin felt more elastic.

As she crossed the room to the shed door, her feet felt so light that she jigged a few steps, like a young girl.

In the shed, with her forehead resting on the cow's warm flank, a joy of life welled up in her and for the first time in years, she broke into song, to the steady rhythm of the milk hissing into the bowl.

'Give o'er thy milk now, m' beaut'ous Bess,
   Give't sweet o'er to me, m' dearie brun cow,'

She had forgotten the rest of the words, so she sang what she remembered over and over in a drone, until the milking was done.

*   *   *

Tek had noted, with unmitigated relief, the better color in Phoebe's face when she woke up. And he had not missed her odd little dance steps as she went out to get the bess's milk. He had an inkling of how wonderful the rejuvenation must feel to her, and did not begrudge that her ailment was curable. He watched the transformation with some longing, though. He knew of no brew that could do the same for him.

The old woman would need some more of the brew every few days, to maintain its effects. Fortunately, the exact dose would become less critical as she adjusted to it and regained strength. It would not be difficult to show her, with Nika's help, how much was enough, and how much would kill her.

When her vocalization floated in from the bess's space, he sighed to himself at the strangeness of it. It grated on his ears. It did not have the flow of a proper song, such as the People sang during their ceremonies.

But when the old woman brought the milk bowl in and set it by the hearth, Tek noted with surprise that it was noticeably fuller than he had ever yet seen it, and he wondered if the woman's odd warbling could have had anything to do with it.

*   *   *

On the second of the four days of seclusion, Nika attempted to fly.

She did not succeed. The sprained sinews of her wing shoulders had not healed enough, nor had the bruising and tears in the muscles between her chest and wing elbows. But it did her good to fully flex

106

her wings, out and then back again, many times over. Her head ached, and her neck felt dangerously frail. She understood that her neck was badly strained. She moved it only gingerly, and had to hold her head to one side.

With her wings stretched out, she was able to use them somewhat like crutches, to hop short distances on her good leg. She knew she had to move herself about, to help with the healing.

It tired her quickly. While she was resting near mid–morning, Phoebe talked to her, explaining that it was Klur and his daughter Ruth who had brought her here, and provisioned them. Phoebe then told Nika that when the Tutners came to claim her, she should hide from them, in her owl shape.

"For I be thinking," she told Nika simply, "that if the Tutners take you away with them, they will not properly care for you. And further, you should never go back to them. For they use you ill, and as a were–owl, you have the means to escape them, and to fend for yourself."

Phoebe promised to help her, first by telling the Tutners that Nika had run away before the storm, and then by helping her hide from them, until she could leave the valley to find some of her own people.

Nika marveled. Not only did Phoebe have health and a spryness that Nika had never seen in her before, she also had no qualms about crossing the Tutners, or violating Nika's indenture. At one point she called Nika 'daughter', which was a balm on Nika's soul.

Phoebe told her to think on it all, and that perhaps they could talk about it on the morrow. She told Nika that because of the depth of the snow, the Tutners would not come until the morrow at the earliest, and that it was more likely to be several days hence.

Nika shapeshifted back to being a girl. She found that it did not hurt as much as it had the previous day, though it was still very painful.

"Phoebe, it gladdens me to see you well again. But . . . your good health . . . will not be pleasing the Tutners. Jacob expects to have your property when you die, which they be thinking will be soon, and he has promised it to Carrie, to sweeten her for marriage. This is well known to me — Jacob and Carrie have discussed it often and . . .

openly enough to be overheard, and understood. And . . . you have seen how Carrie acts when she is here — like it is already hers. And . . . she need be marrying . . . soon."

"Need to . . . soon? Oh. You mean she be with child?"

"Aye. I be thinking so, as do some others. But now that you are better . . . I fear . . . what the Tutners might do."

There was an uncomfortable pause. Phoebe could see that Nika had more to say, but was not sure how to say it.

Phoebe spoke. "It does not surprise me that the Tutners expect to take my property by law when I die, since Jacob is my closest kin. I have not minded this, until fairly recent, when Carrie began to take my belongings whenever she came here. Even then, it only irked, for I have no one to leave my property to, whom Jacob would allow to keep it. I be certain he would raise all manner of objection, if I was to will it to anyone other than himself.

"I think I know my relatives well enough, though, to rest easy. If Carrie needs a marriage portion soon — why then, Jacob can give her some land out of what he already has. He has so much good land — more than enough for two good–sized farms. And then later, after I go, mine could go to one of his younger children."

Nika felt she knew the Tutners better, and was worried about what they — particularly Carrie — might do to gain what they had come to think would soon be theirs by right. But there was nothing specific that she could say against them — nothing that matched her fears for Phoebe.

Soon afterward she shapeshifted back into an owl, but not before telling the lynx that she wanted to speak to him later in the day, after she had rested. The lynx nodded his assent.

* * *

It was obvious to Tek that the girl had to spend most of her time as an owl, while she was healing.

He slept, or watched the old woman as she moved about. He accepted the food that she prepared for the three of them. Some of it was made from dried meat, or was mainly bess milk, or was from a grain similar to the maize grown by the People. None of it was as good as the meat of a fresh hare kill, but it was tolerable.

Tek deliberately left crumbs from his meals on the floor, to lure the mice from their holes.

In the early afternoon of the second day, the owl shapeshifted into a girl and talked to him. He did his best to understand what she was saying. She spoke slowly and stopped frequently to ask him if he understood her. By and large, he did understand much of what she was saying. But he wished he could shapeshift back into a boy — or a man as he might be now — so that she could hear him speak, and understand better the ways in which their languages differed.

First she told him her name — Nika, and that there was something she was afraid of, for the old woman's sake. Tek wasn't sure what it was, but it had something to do with the large young woman who had come with Nika to Phoebe's, on the day of her accident, and the young woman's father. Carrie and Jacob, she called them. Tek already knew that there was something odd and unpleasant about the young woman — Carrie — from his own observations of her loud, brittle voice and her snooping ways. Now, it seemed to Tek that Nika was telling him that Carrie and her father were dangerous, and might even try to kill the old woman, to take something from her, though Tek could not understand what it was that Phoebe had, that could be valuable enough to kill for.

Nika then tried to find out as much as she could about Tek. She told him her clan, and then found out his by naming the clans and waiting for Tek's head shake or nod. She then named every tribe that she could think of, and after each one she asked Tek if it was his. Tek recognized the word for the People in some of the names, mixed in with words for things like hills, forests and even flint, but none of it made any sense to him. The People had ever been — simply and only — the People.

When Nika ran out of tribe names she asked whether he knew what a Christian was. The lynx shook his head, and Nika proceeded to tell him something of her own tribe's history, including what had happened to it after the coming of the whites from across the great salt lake in the east. She explained it in the simplest terms, up to the death of her own family, six years previous. She told the lynx that she had been a servant to a white family since then — though she used the word for 'captive' because she knew no word for 'servant' in her own language. Then two days ago she had been hurt in an accident caused by one of the whites. She ended by telling the lynx that she was not going to be a captive any longer, and that Phoebe had promised to help her to hide, and to escape.

Tek could not understand everything that Nika told him, but he understood enough to know that the People — his People — no longer lived in the forests around here. He also thought that it was right for the girl to escape from the whites, if she could. And he was determined to help her.

It saddened him, to learn that the People were largely gone from these lands. He wondered if the spirits had deserted them, or if the spirits had gone with those that were left when they went away, as Nika told him, to the west and the north.

Chapter 8

That second day ended with an unexpected visitor.

She arrived shortly after dark. They had just supped. Phoebe had not heard anyone approaching, but the lynx got up and moved toward the door, and the owl turned its head to the door and emitted a sharp kweeek.

Before long there was a rap on the door, and a voice called out, "Phoebe, it's me — it's Ruth. May I come in?"

Phoebe replied, "I be coming, Ruth," but then she whispered to the owl, asking Nika if she should hide her, and if Nika thought that the lynx should hide too.

Nika was already shapeshifting back into a girl; when she could speak, she whispered, "No, I'll not hide from the Klurs, at least not in this form. I think I must trust them. As for the lynx — I'll ask it if it wants to stay in the cow shed while Ruth is here."

When she did so, the lynx stayed put.

Phoebe tucked some coverlets around Nika and opened the door to Ruth.

Ruth came in wearing indian snowshoes, with a large pack on her back. She slipped the pack off and bent to unlace the shoes.

Within moments of her arrival, Ruth's dark, quick eyes took in that Phoebe was looking remarkably well, and that Nika was better than she had expected her to be — though she held her head at an odd angle. Ruth also noticed that the creature she had sensed on her last visit, hiding in the loft of the cow's shed, was now calmly out in the open, and was a lynx.

She had brought more food. After she and Phoebe put it away, Ruth sat down by the hearth, and gave her attention over to Nika.

Ruth had some skill with the healing of bones, though she kept it quiet, cautious of backlash from those who might blame her if the patient could not be cured. With some such qualms, she offered her help now.

With Nika's permission, she first moved the coverlets off the girl's injured leg, to examine it.

The leg was bruised, but the swelling was down, except at the ankle. Ruth did not think that the ankle was dislocated, but it surprised her that there was no splint on it. Tactfully, she asked Phoebe whether she thought the lower leg ought to be splinted, to keep the ankle immobile.

There was an awkward pause. The lower leg had in fact been splinted whenever Nika was an owl, with a loop in the tie for Nika to release it, whenever she needed to change into a girl. Now Nika simply told Ruth that her ankle had been splinted most of the time, and that she and Phoebe would now appreciate it if Ruth would show them her way of splinting it.

Ruth did so, and then turned her attention to Nika's neck. Although her touch was delicate, Nika stiffened and cried out. Ruth continued to probe, gently but searchingly, while saying soothing, reassuring phrases.

When she was done, her face was troubled. "I can feel that one of your neck bones is out of its proper place," she told Nika. "I can try to move it back into place, but I . . . may not be able to. And if I try it and fail, Nika, the pain will be worse and . . . you may lose the use of your limbs. Or you may die."

Nika considered, and then asked Ruth if her neck would have to be kept very rigid and still for a long time to heal. Ruth replied that it definitely would.

Nika was silent for a while longer. At last she looked up at Phoebe, and over at the lynx, which was standing nearby.

Then Nika did something that Ruth thought was rather curious. She spoke in another language, and it seemed to Ruth that she was talking to the lynx. She spoke very softly and, Ruth thought, with tenderness. Odder still, several times the lynx seemed to bob its head, as if it had understood her.

Ruth had some questions about this lynx that she wanted to ask, but she had put them aside for later. Watching the girl talk to the lynx now, in a language that Ruth thought was probably Nika's native language, gave her a shiver.

Nika turned to her and said, "I would like you to try to fix my neck, but there is something I must tell you first."

Nika told Ruth that she could change herself into an owl, and that as an owl she had been healing much better and faster, than as a person. She asked if Ruth could fix her neck while she was a person, and then splint it after she changed herself into an owl.

Phoebe spoke then, telling Ruth that what Nika said about being a were–owl was true.

Nika and Phoebe fully expected Ruth to be incredulous, but she did not seem to be the least bit surprised. Instead she said matter–of–factly to Nika, "First I will try to fix your neck. If I can do that, then yes, I will try to splint your neck while you are an owl. But you will have to keep your neck very still while you are changing from a person into an owl. Do you think you can?"

When Nika replied that she thought she could, Ruth simply replied, "Then we shall begin."

Ruth gathered some things she would need, and then very carefully turned Nika over onto her stomach, making pads for her chest, head and neck, to keep her neck as straight–aligned as possible. Her neck would not go completely straight: it twisted slightly to one side, where the bone was out of place. Ruth positioned Nika's neck with extreme care, knowing that if it turned too sharply or the wrong way, the dislocated bone could slip further out of position, damaging or snapping the nerve. From a subtle feel and noise of grinding as Nika's head was being positioned, she marveled that Nika was not already worse than she was.

Phoebe assisted in positioning Nika as Ruth requested. Then Ruth had Phoebe put her hands along each side of Nika's head, to hold it still, while Ruth kneeled over Nika's back to keep her from moving. Ruth then carefully, delicately felt the shape and position of each vertebra in the neck, one last time. Her eyes were closed. She did everything now by touch and feel.

She told Phoebe to brace herself to hold Nika's head very still, but to allow it to shift to a straighter alignment if that became possible. She readied herself, and then pressed her fingers into the

113

place in the column of Nika's neck bones, where she could feel by the rise of one bone that it was not in its proper place. She pressed firmly, and held her fingers there for agonizing seconds as Nika's body convulsed and she cried out, and the neck bone under her fingers did *not* move in the way that it needed to go. Ruth dared not press harder, and she dared not let go. She began to pray, "Our hallowed Father, who art in —," . . . when under her hands Nika gave her neck a sudden jerk, and Ruth felt the bone move as it needed to go. She exhaled the breath she had been holding and said, "It is done! Now all must be still."

She soothed Nika, who was trembling, telling her to calm herself before trying to change herself into an owl.

Ruth kept her hands firmly in place to brace Nika's neck, until Nika was ready to make the change. Then as Nika changed Ruth adjusted her hold as the neck under her hands and fingers became the thin, more flexible neck of a small owl. With Phoebe's help, she devised a brace to hold Nika's neck immobile. She then re–splinted the injured 'ankle'.

When she was done, she tried to settle Nika as comfortably as possible, saying with a small smile, "Ah, you are a pretty little owl, Nika." But her eyes showed her worry. Nika was exhausted. Her eyes were half–closed and her body jerked weakly. The lynx, which had been pacing while Ruth and Phoebe worked on Nika, came up while they were wrapping the owl and putting it near the fire. The lynx sniffed and nuzzled the owl, and then sat beside it.

Ruth and Phoebe were also nearby. After watching over Nika for a while, Ruth told Phoebe that she would like to stay the night, in case Nika needed her care. Phoebe readily agreed.

The cow was milked, and a meal was prepared for Ruth. Then the two women talked quietly.

They had not done so in many a year. The Tutners had seen to that: they discouraged friendliness between Phoebe and the Klurs, and four years previous they had bluntly told the Klurs that *they* alone would take care of *all* of Phoebe's needs. Any contact by the Klurs would be viewed as a grasping maneuver to take advantage of their elderly relative. The imputation was insulting, but there was nothing the Klurs could do about it. No good ever came of crossing the

Tutners. They were sorry, though, to have lost their friendship with Phoebe.

Now the two women talked comfortably, as though there had never been a gap of years.

Ruth complimented Phoebe on looking so healthy and well, which prompted Phoebe to tell her about the how the lynx had guided her in the preparation of a brew that had strengthened her heart.

"It is not a normal lynx," Ruth commented, looking over at it.

"It be very human–like," Phoebe replied. "It does not understand my words, but it understands Nika when she speaks to it in her native tongue."

Ruth nodded. This was as she had thought.

After a pause Phoebe continued, "I think it may be a were–lynx. But it seems to be stuck as a lynx for the time being. For it dotes on Nika, and I think it would be a person for her now, if it could."

"There is something else that is unusual about that lynx," Ruth replied, "but to explain it, I shall have to tell you of some things that happened many years ago.

"First, though, I would like to know what you think of protecting Nika, by hiding her from the Tutners. We could say she ran away. My father told Jacob that she be badly hurt, but I think we could say she fooled us all by shamming."

In reply, with a small smile Phoebe quoted, 'Good wits, by separate ways, do twine.'

Ruth smiled back and asked, "I hope Nika agrees as well?" and Phoebe replied that she did.

With some diffidence, Phoebe then told Ruth of Nika's concern that the Tutners might try to harm her, since her own death was no longer as imminent as everyone — including herself — had thought. They were greedy for her property, and perhaps were in a hurry now that Carrie was expecting, she explained.

Ruth said gravely, "I be with Nika on this, Phoebe. You should be wary of the Tutners."

But Phoebe could not credit it. "I do not like them, but we are kin," she maintained. "To think that of them, I . . . I would first have to see it in their eyes."

Later that evening Ruth told Phoebe why she felt that there was something more that was unusual about the lynx.

"It has an odor about it, that I can smell. It's hard to describe. The closest I can come to it, is the sharp smell in the air, sometimes, right before a big, fast–moving storm comes through. Perhaps you can smell it too?"

But Phoebe shook her head.

"It is quite distinct to me. It is something I have not forgotten, from when I first smelled it, as a girl, lost in the forest.

"I knew — but to properly explain, I must be going back a little further. You remember as I do, Phoebe, the last of those indian raids? My family lived across the river then. In the earlier raids, we'd left our farm for the fort in the town. But that last one caught us unawares.

"For us it started just before nightfall, with the dogs barking. We had only three dogs then. They were quickly shot dead with arrows, and the house was set on fire, with us in it. My parents tried to shoot at them, from the windows, but it was too dark, and they were too many.

"Eventually we had to run out of the burning house. My father went first with his musket, trying to clear the way for us, but he could barely see in all the smoke. They grabbed his musket and knocked him down. My mother, my sister and I were seized and made to go off with them. My mother carried my baby brother in her arms.

"We were taken across the river, and we travelled all that night. The woods were full of raiders like the ones who had us. It seemed that everywhere there such shouts, and screams, and ungodly howls. And smoke and murky shadows from fires of burning farms. Several times we were stopped and guarded while some of the raiders left to attack another farm. Then after a few days it was nothing but trudging northward through the woods."

Phoebe had lived through the indian raids as well, though she had never been carried off as Ruth had. Each time she had gotten away in time and hid in the woods.

"We were being taken through the mountains up to the far northlands, to be sold as servants there. But I was not as securely tied as the others, and on the fourth night I got loose. I did not want to leave my mother and the others. But mother bade me.

"I was not very far away when I heard shouts behind me, with my mother's voice mixed in, warning me that they knew I was gone, and were coming after me. I went to earth in a dense willow thicket and hid until daybreak, and then for a long time after that, until I was sure that they had given up looking for me, and had moved on.

"When I came out of hiding it was colder, and I was in a vast forest alone. I tried to follow the path back the way we had come, but an early snow came through that afternoon, and I lost my way in it. After that I looked for a stream to follow southerly, hoping to find my way down to a settlement, but instead I seemed to be getting further into wilder lands. After a while I found that I was in a place where, for as far as I could see on the slopes all around, there were large black spruces rising up to great heights. And I was sure we had not come through anything like those spruces, when going north with the indians.

"No matter which way I went, I was still under those dark trees. I could not seem to find my way out of them.

"With night coming on, I was afraid of wild animals. Especially wolves. I found a shallow space under a large rock's overhang, and dug it out some more. I fortified it with fallen branches that I stacked up and wedged together. I was tired and hungry and my nerves were frayed, but I still remember how much it soothed my mind, to work on that shelter. I kept at it, just for the comfort of it, long after I thought it was as strong as it needed to be.

"Whenever I found weaker wood, I broke it up and stacked it inside for firewood. Then I got a fire going, and built it up for warmth, and to keep wild animals away. I had found nothing more than a few hickory nuts to eat earlier that day, so I was very hungry. But there was no help for that.

"I slept for a while, but the howling of wolves woke me. They were not far away, and the fire had died down. While I was working to get the fire up again, I heard some strange noises, coming from somewhere up the slope above the big rock that I was tucked under. I have never heard anything quite like it, before or since. The closest I can say is, that first there came a low rumbling like a distant thunder. And then it sounded like something heavy was falling through the branches of the big spruce trees up there, followed by the sound of something landing on the ground with a thump and a grunt.

"Suddenly the forest got very quiet, as if all the creatures of the night had paused and were listening. I listened too, but I could not be still for long, for I had to blow on the fire. If I hadn't, it would have gone completely out.

"I was still blowing on it, adding sticks to it, when I heard a rustling nearby. The rustling got closer, and closer. And just when I had gotten some flame going again, the rustling noise came right up to my shelter, and stopped just outside of it. There was a quiet growly sound.

"That's when I first smelled that odd smell, the same that I can now smell around the lynx.

"I built the fire up, hoping it would keep the animal that was out there, from coming any closer. And for a while it did not come closer. But it didn't go away either.

"Then there was more trouble. There were other rustling sounds out in the dark, all coming closer to where my shelter was. And then yips and a low howling. Some wolves had arrived.

"What happened next . . . I have wondered sometimes, since then, if it was all nothing but a very strange dream. But . . . it couldn't have *all* been a dream, Phoebe.

"The heavy branches I had put across the entrance to my shelter were plucked aside, and a large dark furred animal came right in, and shoved itself right up next to me. It was a bear, Phoebe, about half grown, though it was thin and bony under all of its fur. And that smell — that fresh, storm–coming smell, was all around it.

"I held myself rigid, expecting the bear to attack me at any moment. But instead, it jammed itself in closer beside me, and faced the gap in the branches, where it had come in. I could hear the wolves prowling around outside, and it was not long before one of them put its bold snout through the gap.

"The bear had been very still, but at that moment it roared and exploded into lightning–quick movement. It lunged toward the wolf, snapping its teeth and swiping with its paws, and its roar — Phoebe, its roar was like thunder directly overhead. It deafened, it terrified me.

"I closed my eyes and screamed. And screamed. I could not stop screaming, until I had no breath left.

"When I was finally able to stop screaming I listened, but there were no sounds. It was quiet all within and without the shelter. I opened my eyes, and the bear was just sitting there next to me. So still. So *calm*. The wolves were gone, for the time being.

"The bear was lying on its side with its head up, looking at the fire, just like a person would do. But its head was turned slightly toward me and I could tell, Phoebe, that it was watching me.

"Well, the bear had taken over my shelter, and there was nothing I could do about it. It was not the least bit afraid of the fire, like a wild bear would be. I could not think why it was not afraid unless, perhaps, it had been someone's tame bear.

"It was very cramped with the bear in there. I was wedged in under the rock, between my stack of wood for the fire, and the bear. I had to work very hard to calm myself. I was afraid of the bear, and I did think about trying to scramble past it to escape from it. But I was more afraid of the wolves outside. Very likely they were lurking, somewhere close by in the dark.

"After a while the bear reached across me and with its long black claws it hooked a piece of my firewood from the stack. It dropped the piece of wood close to the fire, and then it nudged me with its paw. When I did nothing, it pushed the piece of wood against the base of the fire, and then it nudged me again, this time much more firmly. Slowly I shifted myself forward, and I put the log onto the fire to burn. Beside me, the bear grunted and nudged me again. I got some more pieces and added them to the fire too.

"The wolves came back a few times that night. I could hear their rustling as they got close, and then their low yips and chuffing as they prowled around, just outside the shelter. But none of them ever put its nose in the gap, like that first one had.

"Whenever they were milling around out there, the bear lay still but alert. At the ready. And each time, after they left, the bear gave a quiet snort, as if to say, 'I knew they wouldn't dare.'

119

"It was around then that I could see there was something about the bear that was . . . humanlike. And from then on, nearly everything that I observed about the bear always seemed to make more sense if I thought of it as if it was human inside — but with ways more like an indian, than like us, Phoebe.

"When day came, we left the shelter. That's when I could really see how extremely thin the bear was. It was hardly more than fur draped over skin and bone. And it moved with an odd stiffness — partly, I think, because it was malnourished. But also, it seemed to be aching. And it limped, favoring one of its back legs. It had a bit of ragged cord around its neck, with a piece of frayed rope trailing from the knot. The knot was loosely tied, and looked as if the bear could simply shift it off its neck, but it never did.

"One of the first things the bear did outside was raise itself up, with its nose high, scenting the air all around. It did that for a long time. It seemed to do it with the utmost seriousness and, at the same time, take a great pleasure in it.

"All that while, I was scouting for a tree to shimmy up. The bear hadn't hurt me when we were in the shelter, but I thought that mightn't hold, once we were out in the open.

"I found a likely tree, and had grabbed a low branch to swing myself up in it. But the bear was behind me with my dress skirt in its teeth, before I knew it had moved. I let go of the branch, and it let go of my skirt. I turned to face it.

"It seemed to really look at me for the first time, since we had come outside the shelter. It sniffed me up and down, and looked over every bit of me, from the top of my head to my bare, cold toes. Its gaze seemed to linger over my face and my hair, and to keep coming back to them. I thought I could read some surprise, and a wonderment, in its eyes.

"Though my hair and eyes are dark, my hair is not as dark as that of any indian I have ever seen. And my skin, even when it is swarthy from sun, does not have the same tones.

"While the bear was looking me over and sniffing me, I was examining it as well. It was a he bear, and though his face was gaunt, its expression struck me as human–like. He seemed to me to be . . . very proud, and his eyes though haggard seemed . . . wise. And I

120

thought, 'This is a powerful beast that must be starving, and yet he did not eat me last night.'

"As I was thinking this, I found that the bear was looking straight back at me. And face to face like that, it seemed to me that he knew what I was thinking.

"The bear then turned from me and simply walked away. And I knew he was leaving that place for good. He would not be coming back. So I had to choose. Should I follow him, or continue on my own?

"I followed him.

"He went on very steadily, out of the spruces and then on until he came to a clearing that was boggy, and full of browned–out cattails. I doubt that I would have found that place on my own. Oh, how I stuffed myself on the root spurs, while the bear ate the roots whole. The bear then went a little further to where water had ponded, and before long he flipped a small fish out of the water, and then another. When he had gobbled them up, he headed straight to where there were barberry bushes growing at the edge of the clearing. We both ate the barberries.

"We went on all day that way. The bear knew just where to go next for food. But he was not wandering directionless. Upslope and downslope, he was always trending southward.

"I could not eat everything that the bear could, but by following the bear I was getting enough to satisfy my hunger. Sometimes I was right next to the bear, eating the same kind of food, but he never drove me off. And when he was moving through the woods, though he did not seem to be paying any attention to me, I think he slowed down for me sometimes, when the going was difficult.

"We reached a dense cluster of oaks not long before dark. There were still some acorns on the ground under them. They were too bitter for me, but the bear foraged for them.

"He found a large cache of the acorns in a tree hollow. He split the tree and began to feast on the acorns that spilled out of it. Two squirrels arrived and chattered angry objections, but there was nothing they could do about the bear eating up their store of acorns. One tried to pester the bear though, with darting rushes. Perhaps it was trying to make the bear leave sooner. But instead it got too close, and the bear killed it.

"I expected the bear to eat the squirrel right then and there, but instead he put the squirrel to one side and finished the acorns. Then, carrying the squirrel in his mouth, he led me to a place on the side of a ravine where the earth was scooped out, forming a small earthen cave. There he dropped the squirrel at my feet and nudged me, as he had the night before. While I gathered wood for a fire, he spent the time with his nose high, sniffing the air.

"It was dark by the time I got a fire going for us. Then I roasted the squirrel on a stick. I had been able to skin and gut it with the sharp edge of a broken stick. While it was roasting the bear kept sniffing at it and looking at it longingly, so when it was done I pulled it off the stick and put it down in front of the bear.

"But the bear did not eat it. Instead, he looked at me and nudged me.

"I picked up the squirrel and pulled off some of the meat for myself to eat. This seemed to be what the bear wanted, because he then ate the rest of the squirrel.

"Other times when I was with the bear, he caught squirrels and other animals, and usually ate them just as they were. But he seemed to sometimes want the taste of cooked meat, and when I cooked it, he always nudged me to have some. That was one of the most human–like things about him.

"After that second night with the bear, time seemed to move . . . strangely. We continued to travel southward, and each day the bear seemed to grow stronger, filling out from his foraging. He moved with ease, no longer limping. All that while I was changing too. It was subtle, but I felt that somehow I was becoming . . . better . . . healed somehow, though I had not thought of myself as ill before. It is hard to describe, Phoebe. I still worried about my family, and I still wanted to get back home as my mother bade me, to help father if he had survived. But while travelling with the bear I felt I had become more of a forest creature like him. I learned countless things from him, and I learned to love the forest, while travelling through it under his protection.

"The weather remained remarkably mild, for late fall. Afterward it seemed that I had been travelling with the bear in the forest for at least a month, in what felt like a never–ending autumn.

"Then one afternoon a huge storm came up. We had been feeling it coming long before it arrived. The skies darkened to near black, and a roaring wind lashed through the trees. The 'coming–storm' smell that I associated with the bear, mingled with the scent of the real storm. The two scents were similar, but I could tell them apart. They were both quite strong just then.

"The bear scooped out a small burrow under the roots of a large tree, and he nudged me to go into it. After I was inside, the bear stood in front of the burrow and worked his jaw and tongue, until he spat something out of his mouth. It was a small piece of stone with sharp edges. With his nose he pushed the stone closer to me, and then he looked at me and made a movement with his head at the stone. By then I had become so accustomed to the bear, that I knew he wanted me to pick up the stone, which I did. It was a nice piece of flaked flint, about half as long and wide as my thumb.

"Heavy rain came down then. The wind was fierce, and there was violent thunder and lightning, like is rarely seen.

"And the bear simply walked away into the storm.

"I knew that the bear wanted me to stay in the burrow, where I would be safe. But I left it and followed him. I'm not sure why I did, except it had to do with the way I felt connected with him by then.

"I was drenched the moment I left the burrow, and the wind was so strong that it nearly blew me off my feet. But once I caught up with the bear and stayed in his wake, the storm was not as violent. All around us everything was blurred in sheets of blowing rain, but immediately around the bear it was much quieter.

"The bear kept going steadily up a long slope, and after a while it didn't feel like we were walking in the forest anymore. It was still raining hard but we were in a fog, and there was a sense of open space all around us.

"Suddenly two great black shapes swooped low over us, with a deafening thunder in their wakes. They were like huge black birds, except they didn't seem to be completely solid. Parts of them seemed to be always dissolving into the wind. They were chasing each other

123

and clacking their beaks at each other, and whenever their beaks touched, there were brilliant flashes of lightning.

"They swooped and circled continuously over the bear, and sometimes they flew close past me in their maneuvers. Their glowing red eyes frightened me — they looked hard at me as their huge feathered heads streamed past — that sight still haunts my dreams, Phoebe, at times, because the look in their eyes was so cold, so careless of life.

"The bear ignored them, no matter how close they swooped. He continued on through the rain and fog. Eventually they wheeled away and did not come back.

"We were in the forest again. I could not see it in the fog, but though the rain had stopped, I could hear it dripping from trees overhead. That was when I heard the sound of something approaching us on both sides.

"Out of the fog on my left came a huge wolf that walked apace with the bear, but a few steps behind it. From the right came an enormous panther, which did the same on that side. Each of them had a ragged loop around its neck, with a bit of frayed rope trailing, like the bear's.

"They ignored me, and the bear ignored them. He just kept moving ahead on his journey.

"Sometimes I thought I heard something behind us, quietly following us, but it was too far away in the fog for me to be able to see what it was.

"We continued on a little further, until we reached a place where the land rose steeply. There the panther leapt up the slope and the wolf followed it, casually going out ahead of the bear. Here the bear paused and scooped out some earth at the base of the slope. I stood close by him, but he never looked at me. Then the bear started up the steep slope, and that's when I could no longer follow him. Each time I tried to scramble up the slope, I lost my footing and slid or rolled back down. I tried so hard to follow the bear up that slope, but it was as if something enveloped me each time and forced me back down. I called out to the bear, to wait for me, but there was no pause in the sound of him and the others going away, further up the slope. It wasn't long before I could not hear them at all.

"So there I was, I knew not where, and alone. The rain had stopped, but there was still a heavy fog. Night was coming on. I crawled into space that the bear had scooped out at the base of the slope, and I slept.

"When I woke, it was morning, clear and much colder. The slope was there, but it did not seem nearly as steep as before, and it did not have anything like the same feel about it. I climbed up it without much trouble, and when I got to the top there was a flat table of rock, and crags on the other side of it. From up there I could see far into the distance. There were pockets of cleared fields, Phoebe, and beyond them, the river. As soon as I saw the river, I knew I was back in the general area of home.

"It took me two days to find my way home from there. I thought that, altogether, I had been gone for well over a month, because I remembered seeing, on clear nights, the changes in the moon, for at least a month. But when I was reunited with my father, he showed me, by the calendar, that I had only been gone a week."

Ruth was silent for a while, remembering. "Yes, time moved strangely when I was with the bear."

She looked over at the owl and the lynx, and saw that they were looking back at her. The owl's large eyes seemed . . . thoughtful, and the lynx . . . inscrutable.

"You should be sleeping, Nika," Ruth told the owl.

"And you," she said to the lynx, even though she knew that it could not understand her. "You have the same scent about you, as that bear had."

She went over to where she had left her pack, and brought it to the hearth. From a pocket sewn into the inside of it, she brought out a small cloth bundle. Unwrapping the bundle, she drew out a piece of flint, about half the length of her thumb.

She looked at it, turning it in the fire's light. "I often carry this with me, when I go out alone."

She laid the piece of flint in the palm of her hand, and extended her arm and hand out so that the lynx could see it.

The lynx leaned forward and sniffed the flint. He looked up at Ruth, and then back at the flint. With his paw he lowered Ruth's outstretched hand to the hearth, and he rolled her palm so that the flint would fall onto the hearthstone. Then he worked his jaw and his tongue, until the smaller piece of flint that he'd kept in his mouth fell out onto the hearthstone.

The moment the flint left his mouth, he had the feeling that he could shapeshift again. But he held back. He certainly did not want to shapeshift here, now, in front of these two Others!

He pushed the smaller piece of flint up against the larger one.

Ruth leaned over and with one finger turned the smaller piece over and nudged it up against one side of the larger piece.

"They match," she said quietly. "The smaller piece is a flake off the larger one."

The lynx seemed to be agitated by Ruth's fingers being so close to his piece of flint. Soon after Ruth aligned the two pieces, the lynx growled and swiped its own piece of flint away from the hearth. It got it back into its mouth, into its place between gum and cheek.

Then the lynx circled and sniffed tentatively at Ruth's piece of flint, where it lay on the hearthstone. Once he dabbed at it carefully with his paw, but he recoiled from that, and did not try to touch it again.

* * *

Tek wanted very much to take possession of the Ruth woman's piece of flint.

As soon as she had arrived, he had scented something different about her. Something she carried with her had the same scent as the Sky World where he had freed the caged bear. The scent was in the bag she had brought with her. Later when she took the piece of flint out of the bag and held it in her hand for him to see, he immediately recognized it, both by its shape and by its special smell. It was the piece that he had flaked off along with his smaller piece in the Sky World. He had used it to cut the lashing on the cage that imprisoned the emaciated bear. He had dropped it after that, in the stir caused by the old woman's rumbling words.

He could not imagine how this Ruth woman — this *Other* — had come to have it. Perhaps . . . perhaps it had simply fallen from the sky, and she had found it. But . . . she was not of the People. She had no right to possess something like this, that came from the Sky World of his People.

126

It belonged to him — or at least, it belonged more to him than it did to her.

He was keen to take it from her, but something about it prevented him. There was a warning in it, a warning not to touch it. When he tried to touch it anyway, a crackling charge like a tiny bolt of lightning jolted through his paw. And there was a distant thunder — not audible, but he could feel it in his bones. It was far away, but very powerful. He knew that he must not try again to take the piece back.

And yet, the Ruth woman handled it with ease. After he backed away from it, she picked it up, re–wrapped it and returned it to the pocket in her bag.

* * *

When things settled down for the night, Tek made his way outside, through the bess's space and into a narrow area along its outer wall, where there was less snow under the roof's overhang. There he spat out the piece of flint and was able, at long last, to shape shift into a person. Since his return from the Sky World, it had been the flint that kept him from shape shifting.

He could feel that he was a man now, instead of a boy. He could see his body, to some extent, in faint moon glow off the snow. He was a very old man. His flesh was withered and his bones ached, much more than when he was in his lynx shape.

He did not know what had happened to the rest of his youth, or to his prime. He did not know where most of his life had gone. He could only guess that the gaps had something to do with the time spent healing in the bear spirit's cave, and perhaps with the time he had been in the Sky World. Time had seemed to move strangely in both places.

A vast discouragement enveloped him. If it weren't for his notion that the girl Nika needed him, he might have fallen into a dark abyss. Almost everything he had ever cared about was gone. His brother Sho, Tsihi, their child not yet born, and all the others of his People that he had felt connected to — nothing of that was left. And this land was no longer the land of the People. He understood that now.

The abyss tugged at him, as an end to his aches and weariness. But he felt stubbornly that he was needed for something, though he did not know what it was. He shivered, and the involuntary jolt of it reminded him of the feel of the thunder a short while ago, when he had tried to touch the Ruth woman's piece of flint.

He wondered if the great bear spirit might be anywhere close by.

He would have to shapeshift back into a lynx soon, to continue his existence with less pain and weariness. But first he wanted to give the bear spirit a token that he understood, and that he accepted his fate, just in case it could hear him.

In a low, cracking voice, he sang the winter song, asking the bear spirit for strength.

If the bear spirit heard him, it gave him no sign of it. But that was usually the way it was.

He shapeshifted back into a lynx, and put the piece of flint back into its niche in his mouth.

*   *   *

Not long before daybreak on the third day, Tek caught a mouse.

The room had been very quiet. The owl and the two women slept; Tek pretended to be asleep as well. The mouse had crept out several times in the night, foraging on the crumbs he had left closest to the walls. He had not chased it, in order to embolden it. When it was much farther out in the open, and far enough from the safety of its closest bolt hole, Tek sprang and closed on it.

Nika as owl was wakened by the soft thud of the lynx landing on the mouse, and the mouse's cut off cry. When the lynx then brought the mouse to her, her excited chirping noises woke Ruth.

The lynx stood over the owl, looking at Ruth with the limp mouse in its mouth. Ruth sat up on the pallet beside owl Nika, and took the mouse from the lynx. She opened up the mouse with her belt knife and fed pieces of its flesh to the owl, which swallowed them eagerly.

A healthy owl would eat a mouse nearly whole, and later regurgitate a pellet of the mouse parts that it could not digest. But Nika was an injured owl. Fed only the flesh, she was saved from the strain of compaction and regurgitation. When Ruth finished feeding bits of the mouse to the owl, the lynx ate some of the rest of it, and Ruth tossed the little that remained into the fire.

In the morning Nika flexed her wings and hopped around. Watching her, Ruth made adjustments to the neck and leg splints. Around midday Ruth left, promising to return before dark. Phoebe bustled around outside, mashing down snow close to the house, splitting some wood, and bringing in snow to melt for water.

When Ruth returned in the late afternoon, she brought food in the pack on her back, and she carried a young dog in a sling.

"The dog's name is Buster," Ruth said. "I brought him at my father's urging."

Buster went immediately to the lynx, sniffed it bossily, and growled. He showed very plainly that he was not going to tolerate the lynx walking around in the open. This was *his* space now, and his directive to the lynx was for it to cower, and flee from him. The most he would permit would be for the lynx to skulk in a corner.

But the lynx did not oblige Buster. It set itself in a crouch, with fur hackled, claws flexing, and a deep throated snarl. A mad fury shone in its eyes. It was ready to fight until one of them was dead.

The standoff was extremely tense, but brief. Buster chuffed, and turned away. He began to stick his nose everywhere else, though he kept one eye on the crazy lynx. He sniffed everything up close — except the owl. The lynx would not let him near the owl. He had to be content to scent the owl from a distance, for the time being.

Watching the dog and the lynx, Ruth nodded. "Father was right about which dog to bring. Buster is not the strongest or fastest, but he is the smartest."

* * *

By the middle of the night the snow crust had hardened enough for Tek to go out and hunt hare.

Some winter hares were sure to be out and about. With their large, furry feet they could travel fairly easily on a hard crust of snow, and the depth of this snow allowed them to reach tasty branches that were normally too high up. The prospect of feeding well was too tempting for them all to stay inside their safe burrows.

The snow crust also supported Tek's weight, for the most part, when he kept it evenly distributed on his large, webbed paws. He found a cluster of pine saplings of a type that hares especially liked, and scraped out some snow to hide himself, and to protect himself from the wind. Then he waited, curled up and listening to the night sounds, and registering their myriad meanings.

Soon after daybreak his effort and patience were rewarded. He dragged his kill back to Phoebe's little home, and the fourth day there was begun with fresh hare meat for the occupants, including — despite Tek's preference to the contrary — the awful buster.

Tek thoroughly disliked the howler that Ruth had brought with her — the buster, as the women called it. The buster was clumsy and noisy. And though it had been there for less than a full day, it behaved as if it deserved to be in charge, while at the same time it fawned over the women in an unwholesome, disgusting manner.

But Tek tolerated the buster; he thought he knew why Ruth had brought it. The previous day, Nika had told him that she feared what Carrie and Jacob might do to the old woman Phoebe — that they might try to harm her. Evidently, Ruth agreed with Nika, that Phoebe needed protection. And protection — that was the one thing that made the busters of this world worth putting up with.

He was also willing to give the buster credit for being very gentle with the owl, when on the previous evening, it was permitted sniff it close up.

Tek wished that Nika could turn back into a girl and talk to him. He would have liked to hear her speaking to him in her language, which was something like his own. But he understood what the braces on her neck and her leg were for, and that she had to remain an owl until they could be safely removed.

He would have liked to have shapeshifted to show Nika who he was, and to speak to her so that she could hear some of the differences in their languages. But he did not want to do it with the women and the buster around. He would have to wait for a better time.

* * *

The fourth day passed quietly and quickly, overall. The women forked out some of the snow in the cow's fenced area, so that the cow could trample the rest more easily, to move about outside. Inside, Nika flexed her wings and hopped about more and more often, and with increasing stamina. In the afternoon, despite the encumbering neck brace, she scrambled onto the hearthstone and made short glides to the floor. Ruth encouraged her efforts, and by evening, Nika was able to flap and glide safely to the floor from Ruth's lap.

But there was a tension throughout that day and evening. It stemmed from waiting for something unpleasant to happen. It emanated from the two women and the owl. But the lynx and the dog absorbed the tension as well, accepting it as their own. They understood that something bad might be coming. They did not know what it was, or how bad it might be, but they understood that whatever it was, it was getting closer.

Chapter 9

Jacob and Sedric Tutner were in the light sleigh, on their way to Phoebe's. It was a beautiful sunny morning. A light snow had fallen overnight but most of the snow from the previous storm had settled or melted to a dense two feet or so, where it had not been disturbed. Over the past four days the Tutners and the Klurs had mashed down the snow on the roads through their own lands, and on their allotted sections of the main roads through the valley, using their oxen to pull the heavy, rolling logs. Now the valley was connected again with the valleys on either side of it, and with the river.

The turnoff for the path to Phoebe's was along the part of the main road that had been cleared by the Klurs. Upon reaching the turnoff, the first thing that Jacob noticed was that, though the snow on the path had not been broken by oxen or mule, someone had been on the path using indian snow shoes.

Up until then Jacob's mind had been busy with his plans for bringing Phoebe's farm back to life. He could already see himself visiting Carrie in the new farmhouse that he would build for her, where she would serve him his evening brandy, and he would be surrounded by boisterous, frolicking grandchildren.

He had brought Sedric with him to help him bring back the bodies of Old Phoebe and the girl. Surely by now they were both dead.

He did not bring any servants, for he did not want to be observed while he went through Phoebe's belongings. This was strictly family business.

He and Sedric got off the sleigh and led the horse along the unbroken path. It was slow going. He had plenty of time to wonder about those snowshoe tracks. He counted three sets: two going toward Phoebe's hut, one going away. Clearly, the Klurs had been checking on Phoebe and the girl, and it looked like one of them was still there. Perhaps the old woman and the girl weren't dead yet after all.

When he said as much to Sedric, Sedric made no reply. He had surmised that much for himself.

On the one hand, Sedric was glad that before long, his loathsome sister would be leaving the main farm property. They would no longer be under the same roof; he would not have to put up with her and fight with her like before.

But he was jealous that she was going to be set up on such a valuable property as this. Even snowbound, he could see that much of its gradual rise of slope got the morning sun. He judged it very sweet land to cultivate, in the right hands. Carrie didn't deserve anything this nice. But his father had explained to him that it was either this, or carving up the main farm property so that Carrie would have some good land to marry with. *That* Sedric could not abide. *All* of the main farm was going to be *his*.

They were about halfway along when they heard the sound of firewood being split. Not long after that, a dog's barking announced their approach.

Jacob's frown deepened. Carrie had told him that the only animal left at Phoebe's was the cow. Phoebe had never kept a dog, and her old cat had died years earlier.

They labored on. At length Jacob could see the snow–covered roof of Phoebe's hut. The sight of it reminded him of another of his vain hopes, that the hut's roof would have collapsed under the weight of the snow.

They reached the short spur that led to the hut. The spur was visibly trampled, from the hut to where they were standing, and from there on down to the creek.

Phoebe walked toward them from the hut, carrying an ax and accompanied by the dog, which was quiet now. Jacob noted with great surprise that it was Phoebe who had been splitting wood in the dooryard.

She did not look or act anything like what Carrie had described. Instead of a tottering, grey–skinned old woman with one foot in the grave, Jacob beheld a woman that was obviously healthy, energetic

133

and clear–eyed. He also perceived that those clear eyes looked distinctly . . . unfriendly.

Behind Phoebe, Ruth Klur came out of the hut and walked toward them, with a pronounced limp. Apparently, she had some kind of leg injury.

Phoebe spoke to Jacob as Ruth came up. "It's been a long time, Jacob, since you have come here."

"Aye, a long time, Phoebe. But Carrie has been coming in my stead."

"By sending Carrie, you have not been well represented, Jacob."

"Oh?"

"She looks upon my property with greedy eyes, which I tolerated in the past, when I was feeling poorly. But I am well recovered now, and will make some changes. But, enough of that for now. How fares your injured servant girl?"

"My injured — oh, mean you Nika? But — is she not here with you?! For that is why we have come — to take her back with us."

"The girl is not *here*," Phoebe scoffed. "Not since before the big snow. We thought she had returned to you. Where else could she have gone?"

'Where else indeed?!' thought Jacob. He could think of one place where she might be — at the Klurs! And yet here was one of the Klur harpies, boldly acting as if there could be no such thing.

"Klur told me that when he brought Nika here, she was too injured to be moved any further," Jacob said sourly.

"Aye, surely she did seem very bad then, all bruised and cut up. Her ankle had to be splinted, and her neck looked dangerously awry. She seemed to me to be quite helpless. But in the morning when I woke, there was no girl here."

* * *

Before Jacob could reply, Phoebe offhandedly invited him inside to warm himself before he went back home. She knew that he would want to look around, to satisfy himself that the girl really was not in her home.

Once they were all inside, Phoebe asked Sedric to fetch some firewood from the cow's shed. He went willingly, and was gone a long while. When he finally came out with a few pieces of wood, he shook his head at his father, letting him know that he had not found the servant girl hidden in the shed or the cow yard.

Phoebe built up the fire, but did not offer Jacob and Sedric any refreshment. She pointed to the large bag of wool beside the door, and asked Jacob to take it back with him. It was the bag of wool that had been brought to her the day of Nika's accident. She told him that she would no longer spin wool and flax for them, in exchange for food.

She also told him that she was ending their arrangement for her three cows.

Many years previous she had reached an agreement with Jacob for the Tutners to keep two of her three cows in their herd. They were rotated so that she had one in milk with her most of each year. In exchange, the Tutners were entitled to the calves from her cows, except when one of her cows died; then a female calf replaced it.

Now she informed Jacob that she would send someone to fetch the two of her cows that were with his herd. To end the agreement generously in Jacob's favor, she gave her word that the Tutners would have any calf born in the next nine months from either cow.

"So," said Jacob slowly, "you wish to end these arrangements that have been so convenient and suitable for us both, for so many years."

"For several years now I have endured being shorted by your daughter in both arrangements, Jacob. It is primarily for this reason that I do not wish to continue them."

"If you had told me this before —"

"It did not seem to matter much, when I was feeling so poorly, and I make no further complaint of it now. But I do not wish to continue our dealings, now that I am fully recovered."

"So you will deal, instead, with the Klurs?"

"Perhaps. Or I will engage a young family to live here with me and help me restore my farm."

"What?! Indentured servants are not nearly so plentiful as —"

"I do not speak of indentures, Jacob. I mean to make inquiries, and find a likable family for an amicable exchange."

"Strangers will take advantage of you, Phoebe. They will —"

"I be willing to give it a trial, Jacob. That is my choice."

135

There was little more to be said after that. As Jacob and Sedric were leaving, Phoebe asked Jacob when Carrie's baby was expected to be born.

"Ah, so you have been told of that?" Jacob asked.

"Is it not obvious to view?" Phoebe countered. She added, "I hope for her sake that Carrie will make a good wife. You can tell her from me, if you wish, that she can keep the cups and such that she stole — that she took from me, as my wedding gift to her."

Jacob reddened at hearing his daughter being called a thief, but made no reply.

When the sleigh reached the main road, instead of going straight home, Jacob directed it to the Klurs. There he demanded to know whether they were harboring his servant girl. Klur solemnly swore on his bible that he had not seen the girl since he had taken her to Phoebe's. He then led Jacob and his son through his home and barns, so they could see for themselves that the girl was not there. He did not have to do it, but he knew it was the only way they would believe him.

When Jacob reached home, he spoke with Carrie, after making certain that no one was about to overhear them. He told her that their plans would require some adjustments. She had counted on some pullets before they hatched.

Not only did it look like Old Phoebe might live for many more years, she was intent on severing ties with them, and even spoke of hiring some strangers to work her farm with her. They both knew where that would lead. The inheritance they had counted on would be wrested from them, though if it came to that they would not let it go without a fight.

He did not mention what Phoebe had told him about Carrie cheating her and stealing from her. He thought it very likely that his daughter had done both, but he saw no advantage in stirring her temper over it.

Instead he spoke of practical matters. He spoke of carving out a farm for her, from his own property. It would not be as large or as well situated, as the Inheritance would have been. But with a generous promise of livestock, he reckoned that her young man would be willing to accept it as a marriage portion.

136

Carrie took the news quite calmly. She thanked her father quietly, with her eyes cast down. She was a model of maidenly acquiescence.

Knowing her as well as he did, Jacob thought her subdued manner was probably a performance — an entirely fitting one. As much as they both enjoyed plotting and planning the future together, there were some things that could not be spoken of between them. But they both knew, as plainly as if it had been said, that it was all up to Carrie now.

Jacob asked Carrie if she wanted him to talk to the young man for her, about the marriage arrangements he had just sketched out. "Not quite yet," was her subdued reply. He nodded, and a brief, measuring glance passed between them.

He then mentioned that the servant girl had apparently run away. She did not seem to be either at Phoebe's, or with the Klurs. Perhaps, he mused, they would find her body — or its picked over remains — when the snow melted.

Carrie shrugged.

* * *

Earlier at Phoebe's hut, when the dog started barking, Ruth scooped the owl off the hearthstone and hid it in the shed's loft. The lynx went with the owl, settling himself into the fodder between the owl and the loft's opening. Later when a young man came into the shed and popped his head up into the loft, all that could be seen among the depleted piles of feed, was what looked like a large old cat curled up in the gloom, staring back at him, with a growl in its throat. The stranger's head quickly dropped out of sight.

After Jacob and Sedric left and were well away, Ruth brought the owl down from the shed loft and put it beside the fire again. The lynx followed.

Ruth did not limp at all now. Her limping earlier had been a ruse. If, later on, any of the Tutners saw Nika in the distance, she would be limping. So Ruth, by pretending to limp, could claim that they had seen her instead of Nika.

Once the owl was back in its place on the hearth, Ruth urged Phoebe to go with her to the Klurs' farm, bringing Nika with her, to stay there until a family could be found to come and live here with her in the spring. But Phoebe did not want to leave her home, if

Ruth would be willing to stay with her in the interim. Ruth agreed to stay in part to help with Nika's care, and in part to help Phoebe with some of the spring work. Those were her stated reasons. But she also wanted to stay because she was more concerned than before, about what the Tutners might do.

Phoebe had been dreading meeting with her cousin Jacob, but it had gone better than she had expected. He had not given her any of the difficulties that she come to expect from him. After years of accepting the isolation imposed by the Tutners, and accepting as inevitable their family claim and greedy ways, Phoebe enjoyed feeling free to expand her contracted life.

But where Phoebe saw a yoke thrown off, Ruth saw still waters that could be treacherous below their placid surface. Jacob himself might not yet realize it yet, but Ruth felt in her bones that he was incapable of letting a valuable property, long coveted, slip through his fingers. Four days previous, she had been silent witness when he had come to her father's home with his usual bluster and brusqueness, demanding his servant girl. Then this very morning, she had watched him absorb with unnatural quietude, both the loss of the servant girl, and the threat of losing a valuable inheritance, while his son's more telltale face twisted with bitter disappointment, and a smoldering discontent.

And Carrie . . . what, Ruth wondered, would a stymied Carrie be capable of?

But it was plain that Phoebe did not yet see the dangers that worried Ruth.

Ruth glanced down at Nika as owl. Nika had been listening to Phoebe and Ruth talking, watching them with her large dark eyes.

She lay awkwardly on her side with her feathers mused and her splinted leg sticking up in the air. But she quietly endured her ordeal, and every day she got a little better, a little stronger. Perhaps in a week or so, the neck brace and splint could be removed, or replaced with something more flexible.

Ruth asked Phoebe if her thoughts on Nika's future had changed.

Phoebe looked down at the little owl as well.

"I wish I could keep her here," Phoebe said, "But when she is well, I think she will need to be a girl at least as often as she is an owl.

And if she stays anywhere around here, eventually the Tutners will see her, and recognize her. I will try to help her find a home for herself among her own people as soon as she is able to travel, either to the west, or to the north over the old trails."

Nika as owl became agitated. Clearly, she objected to something that Phoebe had said. Phoebe and Ruth soothed her, saying that nothing was decided, and that it could all be discussed later on, when she was better.

* * *

Two weeks passed. A spring thaw came. Snow melted, rain fell, buds swelled. A few green shoots poked through the matted chaff on the ground.

Nika's neck brace was removed, and the leg splint was replaced with a wrap. Within a few days, she could limp on her injured ankle when she moved about as a person, and when she was an owl, she could fly with almost all of her former strength.

She quickly settled in to being a girl by day, and an owl by night, snatching sleep in between.

By day she kept close to Phoebe's hut, ready to hide if Buster's barking alerted them that someone was coming. She helped Phoebe and Ruth with chores, including some brush clearing, to quadruple the size of the ground where vegetables would be planted. Much more food would be needed, for the family that Phoebe hoped to bring here.

By night as an owl she hunted mice, and scouted for danger that might approach Phoebe's little hut.

She had told Phoebe and Ruth that, although she would like to rejoin her own people eventually, she wanted to stay with Phoebe for the time being. Like Ruth, she feared that the Tutners might try to harm Phoebe. She wanted to stay until Phoebe found a family to help her with her farm.

Phoebe assured Nika that she could certainly stay for a while, until she was stronger. But precautions would have to be taken to keep her hidden from the Tutners.

* * *

139

It was the evening after Nika's neck brace was removed, that she spoke quietly to the lynx, while she carded some wool that Ruth had brought over. In the language of her people, she told the lynx of Ruth's long–ago journey with the bear. Whenever Tek as lynx could not understand her, he put his paw on her arm, and she went back over that part with different words. Little by little, he was able to understand most of what she was saying.

Most of the time he sat quietly listening to what Nika was telling him. Occasionally he looked over at Ruth as the amazing story progressed. Whenever he did look her way, Ruth returned his gaze steadily.

Twice during the story he became agitated, and got up and paced.

The first time was when Nika told him of the emaciated bear that, based on what Ruth had described, Nika thought might have . . . fallen from the sky.

Because Ruth was an Other, she did not know the stories of the Sky World, as Nika and Tek did. Nika had surmised that the magical bear had probably come from there. Tek, from his own more direct knowledge, thought so too. In the Sky World, the old crone's rumbling, rolling words would have caused the bear to fall from the sky, just as Tek had. But time must have moved strangely. The Ruth woman had met the bear in the woods when she was a child, and she was now somewhat past full grown. But to Tek, it had seemed that his time in the Sky World had happened only recently . . . but how long, he wondered, could he have been asleep by the high mountain lake? Surely, only one night. Possibly two . . . and yet, the season had changed, and he had felt so much older when he woke up . . .

The second time he was shaken by the story, was when Nika told him of the wolf and the panther joining the bear on its journey through the shifting mists, and of Ruth being able to follow the three of them. It was surprising enough that this woman had, when a child, been sheltered by the most powerful of the four wind spirits. But not only that, she — who was *not* one of the People — had actually travelled with three of the four winds as they journeyed together to the home of the Good Twin.

Every child of the People knew the story. The Good Twin had gone to each of the four wind spirits and, one by one, had caused them to submit to be leashed, for the good of the People. In some of the stories, the four would sometimes go to visit the Good Twin, with their leashes trailing alongside them on the ground. But in Ruth's story the rope leashes were mostly worn away.

Ruth and Phoebe sat nearby, spinning the carded wool mostly by feel, watching the girl and the lynx. They both noted the extraordinary way that the lynx communicated with the girl. This was no ordinary lynx. Any vestiges of doubt that they might have had, were dissipated. This was an indian were–creature, like Nika. Nika called it shape shifting, but to them it was like the stories of were–creatures, brought by their families across the seas.

When Nika at length finished speaking to the lynx, the lynx went over to Ruth. He seemed to want to communicate with her, but could not. Nika asked the lynx a few questions in her language, but she was unable to guess at what he wanted to know from Ruth, or what he wanted to tell her.

Chapter 10

It was the start of the Bud Moon,[6] nearly a month after the logging accident. The night shone with the moon's glow. Nika went out as an owl to hunt. For a while she flew just for the joy of floating on the air. Ever watchful for a hawk that was out looking for *its* next meal, she buoyed on the lift under her wings in the spring air's smooth, gentle updrafts. The earth's long curve in the distance was an exhilarating view, as the treetops rushed below her.

The healing of her body had gone well, though she still had to be careful not to strain her neck. The healing of her heart, was well underway. For the past month she had felt cherished and loved. The last time she had felt anything like it, was before she lost her parents and infant brother to the small pox. The years since then had been filled with sadness and drudgery, relieved only by fleeting moments of happiness. But those grey years of servitude were over.

She tipped her wing to bank down into the trees.

She settled on a tree branch that she favored, and began to hunt, monitoring all the movements and sounds around her. A rich vibrancy filled this night. She was only one of many creatures whose blood was stirred by the potent spring air.

She was on the other side of the creek from Phoebe's hut, well up on the slope where mice were plentiful. They were out foraging, and leaving their mating trails through the leaf litter. The criss-crossing scents wafting along the ground excited them, and made them incautious. Hunting that night was quick and easy for Nika.

She was back on her tree branch placidly digesting her mouse meal, when a lynx passed below, not far from the tree, coming from

---

[6] April, usually

further up the slope. She recognized it immediately as *her* lynx — the one that she knew was a shapeshifter like herself, though she had thus far only seen his lynx shape. She supposed that Phoebe was right — that something — perhaps the burdensome pains of old age — prevented this lynx from assuming his human shape.

The lynx was moving slowly in near silence, placing his feet with care, pausing frequently to listen, look about, and sniff the air. He did not seem to be hunting, but was travelling with the normal caution of a lynx.

Nika followed him; he was going back toward Phoebe's hut, though he stopped at the creek for water. He stopped at the place across from where Phoebe usually got her water from the creek, where there was a small clear area.

When he finished drinking, Nika flew down to him. She landed close by, on the dry top of a large boulder that jutted out of the creek bed.

When the lynx saw the owl, he worked his jaw until he was able to spit his piece of flint out. He tucked it away by pressing it into the mud, and pawed a loose rock over it. Then he shapeshifted to a man, and spoke to Nika.

He had already shapeshifted earlier that night, twice. Now that there was no snow to slow the flight of hares, it was much more difficult for him, as an elderly lynx, to catch them. So he had shapeshifted through to buck, and foraged on the rich, succulent buds of the aspens, further up in the hills where he felt safer. That had filled his belly well enough, but by the time he had shapeshifted back to man and through to lynx, he was exhausted. Each time, shapeshifting seemed to take more out of him than ever before.

Even so, he shapeshifted to man when he saw Nika there as an owl. It was the opportunity he had been looking for, to speak with her.

He told her his name, and that he had come from a much earlier time than hers — a time before the whites had come. He told her that when he was a young man, he had taken two pieces of flint from the Sky World, and that the Ruth woman now had one of them. He wanted it back, because he thought he had been sent here to retrieve it, and to return both pieces to . . . where they belonged.

143

He explained that he was not able to take Ruth's piece away from her. He had been thinking, though, that if the Ruth woman *willingly* gave him her piece, then he might be able to receive it. He wanted to try this, and he asked Nika if she would help him, by telling the Ruth woman. Perhaps, since Ruth had spent time with the bear spirit, she would understand that it was important, to return the flint.

He used as many of the words he had learned from Nika as he could, so that she would be better able to understand him. He hoped she understood most of what he said, because the effort of being in the man shape was exhausting him. His limbs trembled, worse than a child's, and his voice rasped and guttered. He asked her, had she understood him?

Nika nodded. She understood virtually everything he said, and a few other things besides.

She already felt a strong love for and bond with this shapeshifter — this Tek, first as a lynx and now as an old man, even though she knew that these feelings were going to give her another burden of loss to bear, before too very long. For Tek was very old. It seemed to her that Phoebe was right: he was able to manage the infirmities of age well enough when in his lynx shape, but in his man shape . . . he seemed more the shadow of a man, than a real one. His flesh was criss–crossed with long puckered scars, his palsying body was a mass of ropey sinews that connected bone with age–wasted flesh. His dark eyes, intense from the struggle of conveying his meaning to her, shone out of deep hollows in his scarred, ravaged face. His voice was breathy with the effort of forcing air in and out of inelastic lungs.

But even with these debilities, Tek had a presence that resonated deeply with Nika. It made her conscious of a depth of loneliness and a need in herself, that she had not understood before. The loneliness and sorrow of losing her own family had never left her, but now she felt a greater loss and need, that could only be remedied by being with her own people, like this one, this Tek.

When Tek then asked her, if she would try to persuade Ruth to give him her piece of flint, Nika nodded willingly. She would help him as much as she could, and then, wherever he went, she would go with him — as long as he would let her. He might not feel the same way about it, but to her, he was the first member of her new family. She was determined stay with him . . . for as long as she could.

Nika shapeshifted into a girl and was about to ask Tek a question, when a dog's excited barking broke the silence. They both recognized the dog by its bark. It was Buster. His barking was coming from where Phoebe's hut was.

And then as suddenly as the barking began, it stopped.

"Something's wrong," Nika told Tek, and she immediately shapeshifted to owl, launched herself, and flew in the direction of the hut.

Tek sighed, struggled with shapeshifting to lynx, and followed Nika as quickly as he could.

* * *

Ruth was awakened by Buster's loud barking and a rapid pounding at the door. Buster was inside, barking at the door, while a tense, urgent voice spoke through it.

"Ruth, it's me — Hannah. Father is hurt. You must come quickly! Quickly!"

But . . . the voice . . . that was not her sister Hannah's voice. It was . . . different somehow. And why would Buster be barking like that if it was Hannah? This was not his 'someone we know has come' bark — it was his 'not sure but don't like it' bark.

"No, Phoebe!" Ruth called out as she scrambled up off her pallet. "Don't open the door!"

But Phoebe had been fooled into thinking that it was Hannah, and had already released the door latch to let her in.

The moment the latch was released, the door was forced inward with a length of wood that was then tossed away outside. Phoebe was knocked over by the door, and the dog rushed outside. Immediately afterward, the door was yanked shut, and by the time Ruth got to it and tried to open it, she could not.

Two people were outside — Carrie and Sedric — just beyond the dark moon shadow along the front of the house. Both of them wore bulky, heavy padding over their clothing, and both of them had a garrote at the ready.

Buster charged Sedric, who was closest, and bit into his padded arm, but Carrie slipped from behind Sedric and got her garrote tight

145

around the dog's neck. Within moments the dog was choking. Sedric got his garrote run around its neck as well. Buster's legs buckled, and Sedric knelt on him, weighing him down and pulling his wire tighter, until he was sure that the dog was dead.

While Carrie had been rapping on the door and mimicking Hannah's voice, Sedric had tied a long rope to the outside of the door latch, with a wooden flip catch set in the rope. As soon as the dog ran outside, Carrie pulled the door shut with the rope. Then she garroted the dog, and when Sedric took over killing it Carrie tied the rope securely to a post near the door. With the rope taut she wedged the flip catch against the door frame. Now the door was locked from the outside, and the women inside the house would not be able to open it.

Sedric raced to the back of the hut, where he ran a rope through the latch of the cow shed door, and tied it to a fence post there.

He and Carrie had worked so quickly that the first part of their plan had worked flawlessly. The two women were trapped inside the house, with both doors secured from the outside. There was no way for them to get out; the windows were much too small for them to climb through.

Most of the plan was Carrie's, though Sedric, once he saw how easy it was going to be, had contributed several useful ideas — including the garrotes for entrapping and killing the dog.

They had put aside their tiffs and worked together on this secret, foolproof plan. They would end Phoebe's life, since she was an impediment to their future happiness. And Ruth — Ruth must also die because she had foolishly entwined her fate with Phoebe's.

Carrie and Sedric were going to shoot fire arrows into the wood–shingled roof, until the shingles caught fire. From there the fire would quickly spread to the wooden frame and log walls. The whole house would burn down, and the two women inside would be incinerated. By morning, there would nothing left but ashes. The dog's body would be thrown into the fire as well, once the roof collapsed. It would look like an accidental fire had killed the two women, and it could never be traced back to them.

After her work on the front door Carrie sheltered behind a woodpile in the dooryard, to get everything ready for the fire arrows.

She and Sedric had decided to work from behind this woodpile as a precaution, because of Old Phoebe's musket. Just in case one of the women managed to load it and get its powder to flash — it was unlikely, but Carrie and Sedric did not want to give them an easy target. The woodpile would protect them.

Carrie hunkered further down behind the woodpile when one of the women broke out the glass of the front window of the house — they might try to fire Phoebe's old musket, after all.

Ruth called out Carrie's name and shouted, from the window, "We know it's you. You mean to burn us up, don't you? But you must not. You must stop this at once!"

Ruth's voice shook, but there were no hysterics. No pleading.

Carrie and Sedric had agreed to ignore anything the women said, but Carrie could not resist mocking Ruth. She sarcastically mimicked her.

She had put her head up, for her voice to carry. Before she finished her taunt, there was a flash at the window and the whizz of a musket ball.

But the ball did not pass anywhere close to her. After a momentary startle, Carrie laughed with a giddy glee.

When Sedric arrived, she told him how wide the shot went and crowed, "Didn't I tell you?! Pathetic old women! Neither of 'em could hit a haystack."

"Still better be careful though," was Sedric's ponderous reply. "Just in case."

They untied each other's bulky pads, and shoved them out of the way. They no longer needed protection from the dog, and would move more easily without them.

They quickly finished the preparations, emptying their bladder of pitch into a wide bowl, and rolling the wads next to the arrow tips through the pitch.

While they were doing this, there was no noise from the house, and no light coming from inside it. They looked up occasionally, but the front of the house was dark in moon shadow. It was hard enough to see where the window was, much less whether there was a musket barrel protruding from it.

When the wads on several of the arrows had soaked up enough pitch for lighting, they each chocked an arrow into their bows, and lit the wads from a candle stub. When the wads blazed with fire, they both jumped up and ran parallel to the front of the house, shooting their arrows low into the roof. Running the length of the house was travelling across a musket's path, making them harder to hit. Just in case.

They turned after firing and looped away from the house to return to the woodpile from a safer distance. A musket did fire from the window on their return trip, causing them to widen their loop back, but neither Carrie nor Sedric heard the ball's whistle, so the shot was not even close. Carrie's confidence, already high, soared.

They were nearly to the woodpile when a fire blazed up there, and they could see that someone was crouching beside the fire! It was incredible, but one of the women must have gotten out of the house, and had lit their bowl of pitch! Before either of them could slow their rush toward the woodpile, the bowl rose and the pitch was flung at them.

The burning pitch splattered across Sedric's jaw, neck and chest. A gob of it hit Carrie's forehead and ran down her nose. Some of it caught her hair on fire.

They both cried out, and dropped and rolled in the dirt to put the fire out.

When they were at last free of the flames and able to notice what was going on around them, there was only moonlit darkness, and a tapping sound coming from the woodpile.

The two arrows they had shot were no longer burning, and there was no other firelight anywhere that they could see.

The tapping was the sound of a musket barrel being knocked against the bowl that had held the pitch.

Though the full moon had been setting for a while, there was still enough of its glow for them to see that Phoebe and Ruth were standing at the woodpile, watching them. Ruth held the musket. Phoebe, a bucket.

Carrie and Sedric, both sitting on the ground, assumed that the musket was loaded, but . . . was it cocked? And even if it was . . . a glance passed between them. They were close enough that, with a little misdirection, they could rush the women and grab the musket, before it could be raised and fired.

Sedric lowered his head and shook it, as if he was dizzy and confused. "How . . . how did you get out?" he asked, slurring the words. Beside him, Carrie rocked herself and whimpered.

Ruth answered him, though he didn't deserve to know. "Shot your rope that held the door," she said grimly. "From the window."

Sedric rolled a little toward the women, as if he was woozy and was only balancing himself to stand up. Carrie also began to stand.

"Stay down!" Ruth spat. But Sedric leaned as if he was about to fall forward, and then he charged Ruth. He had his garrote ready. Carrie did not have hers but she charged in right behind him.

Ruth did not have time to cock the musket and bring it up to fire, but she stepped in front of Phoebe and held the musket like a long bar in front of her, one hand at the head of the stock and the other on the barrel. At the last second she lunged forward, to keep Sedric's charge from knocking her backward into Phoebe.

Sedric reached forward to loop his garrote around Ruth's neck, but she brought the stock end of the musket up between them so that the wire could not fully close around her neck. Then she pushed against Sedric and stomped down on his foot as hard as she could.

Carrie rushed up beside Sedric to get Ruth on the ground by pushing her sideways. But she suddenly found herself blinded by ashes thrown in her face.

The bucket in Phoebe's hands had not held water, as Carrie had thought. Instead it was about half full of ashes. Phoebe had been looking for a chance to sling the ashes into Sedric's face, but when Carrie rushed up she threw it into Carrie's face instead. Carrie also felt the bucket hitting her head, harder than she would have expected an old woman like Phoebe to be able to wield it. Blinking furiously to clear her eyes, she reached out to hit at or shove any part of either woman that she could reach.

She became aware that something behind her was biting her back and buttocks, and tearing up her calves and the back of her thighs with deep, rapid claw strokes. When she twisted around to fend off the snarling creature, she got the front of herself bitten and clawed as well, until she curled herself into a ball on the ground and held herself still, as Phoebe was shouting for her to do. Whenever she tried to uncurl herself, she got bitten and clawed some more, or clouted with the bucket.

Now when she whimpered, she was in earnest.

In the midst of all that was happening to her, she heard Sedric cry out in pain, followed by a dull thud, and then she heard his heavy tread running away, lurching and stumbling. Soon after that she was blindfolded, and tied up. A musty cover was thrown over her, where she lay on the ground.

Neither Ruth nor Phoebe spoke to her, and though she occasionally heard the murmur of their voices, she could not hear what they were saying to each other.

* * *

Sedric had released his garrote when he saw that the musket barrel blocked it. He threw it aside and reached past the musket to throttle Ruth with his bare hands.

There was a sharp pain in his foot, at about the same time that an owl came out of nowhere and bit one of his outstretched fingers, while raking the back of his hand with its talons.

He cried out and staggered backward, shaking his hand to dislodge the owl. He brought his other hand over to clobber it, but the stock of the musket, swung at him by Ruth, connected squarely with the side of his head.

He distinctly heard breakage in his cheek bone as the stock hit him, and then his jaw exploded in agony, the like of which he had never felt before. There were star–like flashes of light, and his brain felt . . . scrambled.

He reeled away. He was peripherally aware that Carrie was being attacked by a wild animal, but he had too many problems of his own to help her. He ran.

His injured foot slowed him, but he had nearly reached the main road, when something thudded past him. It came up and passed him so quickly that he could not guess what it was. Maybe a horse?

After it passed him, it slowed and turned to face him, and he saw in the moonlight that it was *not* a horse. It was a large, gaunt buck.

The buck barred his way. When he tried to go past one side or the other of it, it reared and slashed at him with its front hooves until he had to back away.

He was desperate to get past it, to get away! He searched the ground for some rocks to throw at it. But before he was able to pry any out of the mud the buck rushed him, and kicked his arms so hard that soon the last thing he wanted to do was to pick anything up. The buck then stood over him, and kicked at him until he understood that he was not to move at all.

They stayed that way until Ruth came up with some rope to tie his arms to his sides.

"You're to come back to Phoebe's with me," Ruth told him. "And I give you fair warning. If you try to hurt me, or try to escape, this buck . . . well, he will probably kill you."

* * *

Sound asleep, Klur was woken by a soft but insistent voice, telling him that he had to get up and do something for his Ruth. When he opened his eyes, he saw that the candle at his bedside had been lit, and that the girl Nika was standing beside his bed, wrapped in his spare coverlet.

Klur bolted up in bed and rubbed his eyes. When Nika could see that he was fully awake, she told him that he had to go fetch the sheriff, and she explained why.

When Klur left on his journey it was an hour before daybreak. The moon had set, but the sky was clear and there was enough of the early grey of dawn for him to get a fast start. He ran his horse at a fast trot or a gallop most of the way. He took two of his dogs, running alongside. Normally they were noisy dogs but the pace was too quick for them to have much breath for barking.

He made good time. It only took him two hours to reach the sheriff's house, three valleys over to the east.

* * *

Joshua Gleber was a crusty old bachelor who had been the sheriff for nearly sixteen years. First appointed to the office when a young man, he had been re–appointed time and again because he was known to be a principled man, and because his area was too much in the backwoods to be a lucrative appointment for ambitious, well–placed men. From his first day in office all those years ago, he treated all comers fairly, and acted quickly and decisively to check the lawless, so that decent folk would have a chance to live in peace, and to thrive. Through all those years he had been a diligent, dedicated public servant, but at some personal cost. Between his sheriff work and the demands of running the family farm, he had never found time to go courting.

His area was not as lawless as the one across the river that included the port town. But it still had its pockets of thievery, its flare ups of mayhem. A fair amount of the sheriff work was mundane, but he had faced extreme danger, and grappled with death and suffering — much of the suffering essentially needless, he felt, if only the people involved had been more humane with each other.

He sighed to himself when, though it was still early morning, the dogs in his dooryard started up their barking and surged to the front gate. There was so much overdue field work that he had hoped to get done today. But when he rounded the house from the barn and saw the mud–splattered horseman at his front gate, his many years of sheriffing told him that some — perhaps much — of his farm work would have to be put off to another day.

He did not know the man, but that was a good thing. It meant that the man kept himself out of trouble.

The man gave his name as Klur.

The sheriff didn't know the valley where Klur lived very well. It had been one of the quieter places in his territory. Until now.

He sized Klur up as he listened to him, taking nothing that he was told on faith. He would have to go and look into the matter for himself. But the 'sixth sense' he had developed in his sheriff work told him that he was going to find that this man Klur was telling the truth. On the strength of that, he chose to take his long wagon, rather than going on horseback.

He called in two of his men and went back with Klur, arriving at the turn off to the widow Phoebe's home by mid–morning. There Klur left him, to go back to his own home, while Sheriff Gleber and his men took the turn off. The wagon rattled down a long, overgrown path, past brushy overgrown fields.

They found the spur that led to the home, as Klur had described it, right before the land started a long slow slope down to a creek.

When they pulled up in the yard, there was a woman sitting on a stool with a musket across her lap. On the ground near her lay a buxom girl and a heavy–built young man, both of them trussed up and blindfolded.

Sitting on the ground next to the woman was what looked at first like a large cat, but as they got closer the animal stood up and went with a slow lope behind the house. When it was up and moving, Gleber could see that it was actually a wild animal — a lynx.

The woman's name, he learned, was Ruth Klur. He immediately liked her, though he was careful to put aside that first impression, to be completely neutral in his work.

A much older woman came out of the house — Phoebe Carr, her name was. She also made a good first impression.

He separated everyone. Then he had Ruth and Phoebe, each in turn, show him where and tell him what had happened, all the while asking his questions.

Both women were obviously strained and tired. But even in the aftermath of what had happened to them, and still surrounded by the detritus of the struggle, they assisted him with a quiet resolve that spoke well of them. These were not hardened, callous women, like some he had met in his work. He discerned in a multitude of ways that they were both, in fact, very sensible and caring.

After he had gone through everything with them, he questioned Carrie and Sedric, also separately.

Carrie denied everything, and claimed not to know how she had come to be there, until he had her stand up, and showed her how obvious it was that one set of the pads had been made to fit snugly around her extended belly. Then she admitted to everything that she and her brother had done, but she insisted that her brother had forced her to help him. She had complied because she was terribly afraid of him. She said she could not be blamed for *anything*, because she had been *made* to do it.

Questioning Sedric was difficult. The young man could barely speak, because of his broken jaw. But in what he *was* able to communicate, in mumbled one and two word answers, it seemed to

Gleber that Sedric was being truthful, if only because his head was paining him too much for him to be able to concentrate on lying to anyone, about anything.

In deciphering Sedric's answers, it helped that they were corroborated by what Ruth and Phoebe had already told him.

Sedric admitted to killing the dog, and to his part in trapping the two women inside the house, in order to burn them up. He admitted to trying to strangle Ruth after the women escaped from the house. And he answered 'yes' when asked if he had done it so that his family would get Phoebe's land. But he vehemently denied that it was entirely his plan.

A few of Sedric's one and two word answers to Gleber's questions did not make much sense, but none of those related to the criminal acts.

Shortly after noon, Sheriff Gleber put Carrie and Sedric Tutner formally under arrest. He had them loaded into the wagon, along with the nonperishable, portable evidence — the garrotes, body pads, and such. And he had one of his men dig a hole, big enough for Ruth and Phoebe to bury their hapless dog.

Just before he finished his work there, Constance Tutner — Sedric and Carrie's step mother — arrived in a buggy.

*   *   *

Jacob had known that his two eldest children were up to something. Though Sedric and Carrie normally fought each other worse than cat and dog, for the last several weeks they had been the exact opposite of mortal enemies. They had been chummy, whispering together or closeting themselves in an empty shed, or in one or the other of their rooms.

And because neither of them wanted him to proceed with dividing up his farm yet, so that Carrie would have a marriage portion from it, he had a fairly good guess that what they were doing was hatching a plot to kill off Old Phoebe and, if necessary, the interfering, busybody Ruth.

This was exactly what he wanted them to do — as long as they did not get caught. He didn't *really* want to have to lob off a piece of his own farm for Carrie. But as the established, upstanding patriarch

154

of the valley, *he* could not be directly involved. So it was up to them. The how and the when of it — that was entirely up to them.

He expressed no curiosity about what they were planning. He simply expected that, with so much at stake, they would be sure to be careful, smart and discreet about it.

He thought he had heard them sneaking out of the house the preceding night, after he had gone to bed. But he did not get up to check because, he told himself, he ought not to know for certain.

When neither of them showed up for breakfast in the morning, he was not overly concerned.

But as the morning wore on, and it became obvious that they were not at home and that no one knew where they were, Jacob began to wonder if something had gone wrong for them at Phoebe's.

Not long before noon, he decided that he had better find out. He told his wife to take one of her custard pies over to Phoebe.

She asked him why on earth she should take one of her pies to that cranky old woman, who had so recently cut off longstanding ties with them. He told her irritably to go anyway, and say whatever she pleased about why.

She went, and returned after about an hour, with the pie still beside her on the buggy's bench, and wide–eyed with shocking news.

* * *

When Constance arrived at Phoebe's, she was surprised to see a large wagon in the dooryard, and three strange men milling around. She pulled in alongside the wagon, and saw two more strangers tied up in the back of wagon. At least she thought they were strangers, until one of them spoke to her, and she realized her stepdaughter Carrie had spoken, and that the other person in the wagon was her stepson Sedric! She would never have recognized either of them: their faces were all swollen, and had terrible burns, cuts and scratches. One of Carrie's eyes was swollen shut. Sedric's swollen and bruised jaw was crooked. They were both incredibly dirty and bloody, and their clothes were in shreds and tatters.

Sheriff Gleber came up to Constance, introduced himself, and told her what Sedric and Carrie had been caught doing, and that he was taking them to the gaol. He advised her that though the two would receive basic medical care, their father ought to arrange for a doctor to medic them, since they were not paupers.

As soon as the sheriff left with his prisoners, Phoebe informed Constance that she should turn her buggy around and leave as well. Phoebe thanked her stiffly for bringing the pie, but told her that under the circumstances, she would not accept it.

* * *

Sheriff Gleber spent much of the long ride to the gaol mulling over the Carr case.

Many cases had fairly tidy puzzle pieces that fit together reasonably well. But some cases — and this was one of them — had pieces that just weren't going to fit neatly into place, no matter what. Those were the case's misfits.

Misfit pieces were troublesome, but not necessarily fatal to justice. They just meant he had to take more care, to determine whether their odd little gaps could be ignored as minor and peripheral, or were instead signaling that some important parts of the puzzle were not yet set correctly in place.

In the Carr case, he was confident that gaps around the misfit pieces were of the former type — minor and peripheral. The heart of the case was rock solid. He had more than enough evidence that the Tutner brother and sister had by stealth tried to kill two blameless women — one of them their elderly relative — for naught but property gain.

Of *that* he had no doubt. But it was the accounts of how the two women had defended themselves and subdued their attackers . . . that was where the misfit pieces were.

One such piece was that lynx . . . Ruth and then Phoebe had told him that the lynx was just a half–wild creature that Phoebe had tamed, to some extent. They both said that the lynx was very protective of Phoebe. That was supposed to explain the claw and bite marks all over Carrie. But . . . it was so unlike any feline to protect a human like that — even a human it was attached to.

It would be much more plausible if the lynx had attacked Carrie after she had done something to harm it. But there was nothing like that in anything he had been told.

156

Another misfit piece was the extent of Sedric's injuries. Sedric was a big, brawny young man, while Ruth — she was middling tall, but she was not built like a bull, as Sedric was.

So Gleber would have expected Ruth to have gotten the worst of a physical confrontation with Sedric. But though Ruth had some bad bruises and cuts, it was Sedric who had gotten the worst of it by far. Besides his head injuries, he looked like he'd been subjected to a heavy drubbing by someone who was much more his own size and strength. His body was covered with knotty welts, and odd pointy, indented cuts. Gleber was also fairly certain that besides having a broken jaw, the young man's dominant forearm was broken.

Ruth steadfastly maintained that she had merely been lucky in freeing her musket from the garrote, and had swung it at Sedric when he lunged at her. Then when he fled, her story was that she had followed him and whacked at him with the musket until he fell, stunned, and she had been able to tie him up.

He believed Ruth when she told him that she had not hit at Sedric once he was down. He was a good judge of character, and knew that Ruth, even when roused, would not beat a man who was no longer a threat. He would stake anything — everything — he had on that opinion of her.

And he could grant Ruth *one* very lucky swing of the musket.

But her account of pursuing Sedric after he fled . . . Sedric would have rounded on her, and easily gotten the musket from her, with a completely different outcome.

He suspected that there was someone else, someone who had helped the two women subdue Sedric. But both women denied it. And Sedric denied that anyone else was there — though he had been muddled about it. He had grunted something confusing about an animal — a bird, or maybe what he was trying to say was a buck. Gleber could not make any sense of it.

There were some smaller misfit pieces as well — odd pauses, odd phrasing — nothing very specific though.

Like what happened when one of his men was clambering onto the roof. He had asked the man to retrieve the two spent fire arrows that had been shot into the roof. They were part of the evidence that he wanted to take back with him.

Ruth and Phoebe were standing on one side of him; the three of them were watching the man on the roof. Gleber commented about how very lucky it was, that neither of those arrows had actually caught the roof on fire. After a pause, Phoebe reminded him that she *had* managed to sling some buckets of ashes and dirt up there. But her voice sounded a little odd. When he turned to observe her expression, he caught her and Ruth exchanging glances, with grave fleeting smiles. The two women, realizing that they were observed, returned their gazes to roof and murmured solemnly, almost in unison, that yes, it was a very lucky thing.

A small jarring incident. A small, misfit piece.

After he finished reviewing the misfit pieces in his mind, he put them aside and let his thoughts go free, to stretch and ramble. During much of that time, it was the image of those two plucky women, looking back up at the roof, that kept coming back around in his memory.

He smiled to himself.

Ruth and Phoebe had not been completely honest with him. There were some things that they did not want him to know.

But he did not like them any the less for it. They would have their reasons, and he thought he would approve of those reasons, if he ever came to know what they were.

He then thought more about Ruth and Phoebe, as people. He found that he didn't just admire their pluck. He found that he thought highly of them both.

He liked their compassionate natures, and their quiet strength.

He liked how sensible they were. Having had some suspicions of the Tutners, they had tried to protect themselves, by having a good dog and a good musket there with them.

But when their enemy proved to be more cunning and brutal than they had anticipated, he admired how brave they had been — how they had fought back with unflinching courage. Certainly, they had been lucky. But also, they had done much to help themselves.

Gradually his thoughts settled more and more on Ruth. And he began to wonder . . . what she might say if . . .

Chapter 11

Before nightfall, Klur came by Phoebe's hut with two of his best dogs, and his musket. None of them were expecting to have any more trouble with the Tutners, but they were taking precautions. And Klur had judged that one dog would not be enough.

The dog that was best able to tolerate the cosseted lynx — that was the dog that was allowed to be the inside dog when the house was closed up at night. A sturdy shelter for the other dog was improvised outside, next to the front door.

Klur left his own musket with them, and took away Ruth's musket, to repair it.

After he left, Nika came out of the cow shed and let both dogs get used to her. Then she took up her place at the hearth again, to watch over the ailing lynx.

*   *   *

Tek had pushed himself to the utmost that day, even though everything and every shapeshift cost him dearly.

As a lynx he had bitten and ripped at the Carrie woman, keeping her off Phoebe, as Nika had signaled to him to do. When the big, moose–like Sedric man fled, Tek went after him because he had seen the man's massive arm swinging down to hit Nika as owl; the man would have killed Nika if Ruth hadn't hit him first with her magic stick.

Nika caught up with Tek before he reached Sedric and, after shapeshifting from owl to girl, she asked him to do no more than subdue him.

When Nika reached Tek he was still lynx. But he knew he would have to shapeshift through to buck, to go up against Sedric.

After she left him, while he was shifting to his man shape, to get through it to buck, he felt a snapping and crumbling inside himself.

159

The pulses that ran through his body warned him, that he should not be straining himself now. But he could not help Nika if he heeded the warning.

He recovered somewhat while he was buck, enough to capably subdue Sedric. But he was struggling, even as a buck, by the time he got himself back to Phoebe's hut, back to Nika.

Nika had never seen him before as a buck, but she knew him immediately, and could also see something of the struggle to maintain life that was going on inside him. She coaxed him inside, where he collapsed at the hearth. His breathing was shallow. Every part of him felt more deeply hollow and empty, than ever before in his life.

He slipped into a resting daze, covered and kept warm by the fire.

When the light of day came, he had recovered somewhat. A while later, Nika spoke softly to him, telling him that a chief of the whites was coming, to take Carrie and Sedric away for punishment. She explained that this chief would not understand about a buck recuperating in Phoebe's house. They wanted to move him into the cow shed, and cover him over with hides, until the chief had come and gone.

Tek gave himself some time to think, and then he signaled to Nika, to wait a bit longer.

Slowly, painfully, he shifted through to man, and then to lynx.

It nearly killed him.

But he did it slowly enough, and when he was past the man shape, it got a little better. He rested as a lynx, weak and dazed, until Nika spoke to him again, telling him that it was time for her to hide. The chief was almost there. She told him that he could stay at the hearth if he wanted to, but that she would carry him up to the loft over the cow shed, if he'd rather that.

He surprised her by getting himself up, and going outside to sit beside Ruth until the chief arrived. He was determined to see this chief before he went to the loft, where he would try to sleep off his daze and hollowness.

When a big rattling wagon rolled up, Tek had no difficulty knowing which of the three men was the chief. He wasn't the biggest

160

of them, but he carried himself like a chief, and the other two men deferred to him.

Tek found that he was not disappointed in this chief. Yes, he thought, this was a man who could mete out a big enough punishment for Carrie and Sedric.

* * *

Later after the sheriff left, Nika carried Tek in his lynx form down to the hearth where he would be warmer, and could be watched over.

The household settled into a quiet state, to get past the horrors, to settle the nerves. To recover. To heal. The hush of it was broken only by Klur's short visit in the late afternoon, when he brought the two dogs and exchanged muskets.

The dogs were excited by their new surroundings, and by the scent of Buster that was everywhere. But they kept themselves quiet. They seemed to understand that this was not a time to be boisterous.

At night when Nika curled up to sleep beside Tek at the hearth, Ruth brought her some coverlets.

* * *

Nika forced her body to relax, but her mind was unruly. It would not stop running through the recent terrors.

She had shapeshifted to girl and untied the rope at the back of the house, not long after Sedric tied it. She had gone inside to Ruth and Phoebe, and in hasty whispers they planned their defense, and counterattack. Phoebe went out through the back door with her, while Ruth stayed inside and shot through the rope that kept the front door from opening. That gave them both ways out and it was a clever ruse: it kept their attackers from knowing about Nika being there and helping Ruth and Phoebe.

It was Nika who had lit the pitch and flung it at Sedric and Carrie. While they rolled in the dirt to smother the fire on their skin and clothes, Nika shapeshifted to owl and flew to the roof with one of their canvas bags, which she used, when shapeshifted back to girl, to smother the two fire arrows. Then back as owl, she was still on the roof when Ruth drew Sedric and Carrie's attention away from the

161

house, by tapping the end of her musket barrel against the pitch bowl.

When Sedric attacked Ruth, Nika dove down and bit his finger to the bone.

Then came more rush and flurry. She directed Tek to keep Sedric from getting away, and then flew to Ruth's father, slipping in through his open window as owl, to ask him to go for the sheriff.

When it was, at last, all over, she could not settle her overcharged mind. She re–lived the horrors of the vicious attacks. She blamed herself for not convincing Phoebe of the danger. She grieved for the dead dog, and she blamed herself for the toll on Tek.

Her thoughts took on distortions, exaggerating every inadequacy she felt. She fell into a nightmarish abyss, spiraling downward through thin, uneven air.

Air was her medium. Even before becoming a shapeshifter, she was conscious of its weight and depth, and attuned to minute changes in its sweep. Once she was able to fly, air was paramount. Her life depended on knowing how well air would sustain her: would it buoy her, or she would have to beat her wings forcibly against it?

She was deep in the abyss before she began to beat her wings — her spiritual wings. She fought with rapid beat, beat, beat against the thinnest imaginable air — she could *not* have prevented Sedric and Carrie's attack, she told herself sternly. Beat, beat, beat — she could *not* have gotten there in time to save Buster's life. Beat, beat — beating harder still against the light and treacherously roiling air — it was *too soon*, to despair of Tek's life . . .

This last one was the fear that, to save herself, had to be put aside. It was the one fear with the power to thin the air until there was nothing for her wings to beat against. It was the one fear that would cause her to fall.

She fought the insubstantial air — in her mind she continued to beat her wings against it — until at last she found herself teetering on the edge of the dark, sweeping emptiness. It still tugged at her, but she understood it better, and was wary of its pull.

She had done her best with what had been thrown her way. And her best *had* been good, and good enough. She made a little sing–song of this assurance — a little prayer phrase. Unconsciously she hummed it, and murmured it.

Tek stirred next to her. He reached out and put his paw on her arm. His comforting gesture strengthened her assurance, and she thanked him, shyly.

By slow degrees, the torturing whirl in her mind slowed, and at last she rested, body and mind, nestled against the lynx.

* * *

During the evening Ruth and Phoebe moved about quietly, before turning in early.

That morning, they had both been in the house when Nika knelt by Tek, to explain to him their plan to move him into the cow shed while the sheriff was there. They had seen Tek change from a buck into a skeletal, horribly scarred old man, and then from a man into the scrawny lynx they already knew. It had alarmed them both to see how he struggled to breathe and to control his limbs while he was a man. They had both seen enough of the kind of death in which life gutters, to understand that he was gravely risking his life in each of these transformations.

And yet he had taken that risk, several times.

They knew he had done it for Nika, but they were still humbly grateful. Without his help and Nika's, they would not have survived Sedric and Carrie's attack. They would be dead now.

They were more than grateful. They felt they owed a debt to both Nika and Tek.

* * *

The next day, Phoebe, Ruth and Nika did their best to re–establish a sense of normalcy. They did the usual chores.

When Ruth was down at the creek, to get some water, she smelled a waft of the scent that she associated with the magical bear, and with the lynx — the scent from the pieces of flint. She searched until she found the smaller piece of flint that Tek had left across the creek, under a small rock. She took it back to Phoebe's home, and gave it to Tek.

Phoebe, Ruth and Nika worked diligently on cutting and digging the larger of the brush roots out of the new garden plot, so that the ground could be turned when it got a little drier. Tek slept through most the day, and that night.

During a break from their clearing work, Nika related to Ruth and Phoebe, what Tek had told her of his past.

She explained about the Sky World, and the wind spirits, and about how she thought that the bear that Tek rescued in the Sky World, was the same one that Ruth had travelled with in the forest, when she was a child.

She told them about how Tek had freed the bear in the Sky World — by cutting through the lashing on its cage with the larger of two pieces of flint, that he had flaked off a rock up there. She explained that Tek had then fallen to earth from the Sky World with the smaller piece of flint, and that she thought that the bear had fallen too, with the larger one.

They had all seen how Ruth's piece of flint fit exactly with the piece Tek had. They could all agree that the two pieces had started out together.

Nika explained that Tek wanted Ruth's piece, but that something would not permit him to take it. But if Ruth was willing to give it to him freely, he might be able to receive it.

Ruth readily agreed to give her piece of flint to Tek. "But . . . Tek is dying, Nika. What if he dies, either before I can give it to him, or afterward while he is still here with us?"

Nika thought about it. "I am not certain," she replied, "but if that should happen, then I think that we should bury both pieces of flint with him."

The next morning Tek was a little better. He sat up, and drank some water, though his lynx head drooped and bobbed weakly. Nika told him that Ruth had agreed to give him her piece of flint. Would he like her to try to give it to him now? He signaled his assent.

Ruth took her pack down from its peg, and brought out her piece of flint. She ran her fingers over its sharp edges, and along its flat planes. For a few moments she wished that she had not agreed to give up this vestige of her time in the forest, long ago, with the magical bear. But those thoughts were fleeting. She understood now, more of what had been happening then. And she had already decided that Tek had a better claim to it.

164

She set the piece of flint on the hearth stone in front of Tek. Repeating the phrases that Nika spoke to guide her, she did her best with the pitch and aspiration, to tell Tek in something close to his language, that she was freely giving the piece of flint to him.

Then she slid it closer to him until it was only a few inches away.

It was so quiet in the room, that they could all hear the light scraping sound of the flint piece being moved on the hearthstone. But only Nika and Tek could hear the distant roll of thunder, and they could hear it only because it was more like a vibration that they could feel in their bones, than an actual sound.

Tek put his nose down to the piece of flint. It had its special scent, but there was none of the 'no touch' warning about it now. He uncurled a paw, and advanced it to touch it. There was no crackling charge or jolt, so he scooped his paw around the flint and swept it toward him.

It belonged to him again. He had it back.

Later Nika asked him if he wanted her to bind both pieces of flint into some hide strips that she would braid together and tie around his neck, so that he could carry the flint with him that way. He assented, and removed the smaller piece from between his gum and jawline, so that the two pieces could be bound together. Nika joined them and laced them into the hide strips. Then she fashioned the strips into a loose collar, and slipped it around Tek's bobbing neck.

In the late afternoon, the dogs began to bark. Nika hid, and Ruth and Phoebe went down the spur to see who was coming.

It was Sheriff Gleber, on horseback.

He had told them that he would come or would send someone, if he had news, and he did have news for them. But that was not the only reason he came. He had decided to come courting.

He could have sent a boy with the news, but he had 'worked like a demon' to get mostly caught up on his farm work. He wanted his mind to be clear and easy about taking the time off.

He had spiffed up himself and his horse's tack. He was wearing his only suit, and had a small sprig of forsythia in his hatband. He was riding his most presentable horse — a chestnut mare, that he had brushed and combed until her coat was glossy. Ruth was a smart woman. She would know what it all meant.

But the news first.

The law man had presented the case against Sedric and Carrie, and the magistrate had bound them over without bail. In about a month, Ruth and Phoebe would have to travel to the court, to testify at their trial.

He moved on to his other news. He had found a family that he would vouch for, that might suit Phoebe.

It was a man and his wife, with a nearly grown son and a much younger girl. He knew them to be decent, capable farming people, but they had recently lost their farm through no fault of their own. It was on rented land, too near the main town, which was growing rapidly. Their landlord had ousted them and was selling off the land for businesses and homes.

The family had all of its farming gear and livestock, and the man was a good carpenter. But everything they had looked at thus far was either too much or too little — either an expensive, fully stocked farm where their own equipage and livestock were superfluous, or hopelessly rough land rejected by everyone, for good reason. Lately they'd been planning to sell off most of their gear and livestock, and head further west to start over.

Phoebe's farm property was brushy and it needed some buildings, but it was not too far gone. Gleber thought that the family and Phoebe might be able to work out an amicable lease–for–work arrangement if, after they met, they thought that they could get along. On the strength of Gleber's recommendation, Phoebe agreed to let the family come and look the place over.

Gleber asked to see the foundations for the old cabin and barn. With Phoebe and Ruth, he walked through the brush to look them over, and was glad that he would be able to tell the family that the foundations were still in good condition.

Phoebe also pointed out the old well, sour only from disuse. It had been easier for her to take the water she needed from the creek, she explained, than to use the well enough to forestall brackishness.

Gleber then asked to see the size of the vegetable plot that Phoebe and Ruth were clearing.

They pointed it out, thinking he would glance at it in passing. Surely, he would not want to walk into its mire, in his nicely polished boots.

But he went right in to where they had been working, not minding that his boots got mucked up.

They were both sure that he saw the footprints in the dirt, that were much too small to be either of theirs — Nika's footprints. But he did not ask any questions about them. Instead he asked about their plans for the planting, and made a few helpful suggestions.

When they got back to the dooryard, Phoebe asked if she could talk to him privately. Ruth picked up some buckets and went to fetch some water from the creek.

Phoebe explained that she planned to make a formal Will with a law man, when she came to testify in the case against Sedric and Carrie. But in the meantime, just in case anything happened, she had handwritten a Will. Would he be willing to sign witness to it?

He asked her to read the page out to him, but without telling him the names of her beneficiaries. He wanted to hear whether it sounded enough like a Will to be legal. She did so, and it did. He signed and dated it after her, with the top folded over. When the Will was sealed closed, Phoebe asked him to take it with him to the law man she would use for her formal Will. He agreed to do this as well. It was a simple, sensible precaution for Phoebe to take, against her greedy relatives.

Then he went down to the creek to find Ruth. There he asked her if he could court her. And she agreed to give his courting a trial. As he carried the buckets of water back up the slope for her, they felt as light to him as if they were filled with feathers!

He had to leave soon afterward. Clouds had overspread on a cooler, buffeting wind. He was going to have to move along if he didn't want to get caught in the heavy rain that was bound to follow the wind.

He did get home in time, just before dark came and the rain began in earnest, but it was the mare's doing, not his. He was too immersed in fluttering awake–dreams of Ruth filling out the empty half of his life. He was too distracted to keep the mare going at a smart enough pace to get home ahead of the storm. So the mare did it all. She was determined to get back to her nice dry stall before the soaking wet came. She could feel the storm building up behind her. It was not an especially fast–moving storm, but when it arrived, it was going to be a behemoth.

*   *   *

Rain fell in nearly solid sheets.

Lightning split the sky in huge livid fissures, brighter than day.

Thunder boomed and crackled until the earth bounced and trembled.

At Phoebe's, the outside dog was put into the cow shed until the storm's wildness abated.

The storm seemed likely to last through the night, but about mid evening, it quieted suddenly. Abruptly, there were neither rumbles of thunder nor the drumming of rain on the roof. Ruth looked up from her spinning, to comment on it, but she did not speak her thought, because she saw that both Tek and Nika were staring intently at the front door.

"Something . . . someone . . . is coming," Nika said. Her eyes were big and round, as she looked at the door.

When Nika spoke, Phoebe looked up as well. But she was puzzled, because the inside dog had not roused. He was asleep at her feet.

She nudged the dog with her foot. The dog woke, but he did not bark. He got up though and, like Nika and Tek, he stared expectantly at the front door.

Something outside buffeted the door. It might have been the wind, but . . . there was no sound of wind now.

Ruth called out, loudly, "Who is there?"

There was no answer.

She went to the shutter for the front window, released it, and slid it slightly to one side. But she could see nothing outside. "Fog," she told the others. "There's a very dense fog."

Then, "What is it, Nika?" she asked. "Is it . . . is it dangerous?"

"It's . . . it's a presence," Nika replied. "I don't think it will hurt us, unless . . . unless we make it angry. But I've never . . . I cannot be certain."

Ruth caught a waft of scent coming in from the outside. It stirred in her memory: it was the scent of the magical bear.

She turned to Phoebe, and told her that she thought it was alright to open the door. But it was Phoebe's home. It was for Phoebe to decide.

Phoebe looked around at the others.

The last time she had opened the door in the dark, the dog Buster had been killed, and if it hadn't been for Nika and Tek, she and Ruth would have been killed too.

But this . . . this was different. This was . . . a presence, Nika had said.

And the dog . . . the dog was so calm.

Phoebe had just decided to trust the dog's instincts, when the door buffeted with more force.

A presence. Don't make it angry.

Phoebe got up and opened her front door.

A huge nose in a colossal head loomed out of the fog, sniffing — an enormous snout with large sharp teeth showing, and with deep set eyes farther back.

It was the head of a bear. The fog was too thick for her to see the rest of it, but she was sure from the head that it would be the biggest bear she had ever seen.

Ruth came up beside Phoebe.

"Phoebe, that is *the* bear. That is the bear that I journeyed with in the forest, when I was a child."

* * *

Ruth recognized the bear by its eyes. They were intelligent eyes, and just as expressive as they had been years earlier in the forest, when they seemed to be able to 'speak' some of the bear's thoughts to her.

Right now, the bear's eyes seemed to be saying, 'I recognize you too, from before.' There was a pleasantness in the bear's expression, but no warmth. And Ruth realized from this, that the bear was not there because of her, or interested in her.

Looking at Ruth, but with a quick glance over to Phoebe, the bear jerked his head a little. Ruth understood what that meant too, from her time years earlier with the bear.

"He wants us to move out of the doorway," she told Phoebe.

The two women moved aside. The bear did not come in — he was much too big for that. But he fixed his gaze on Tek, and grunted.

Tek came forward slowly. After a moment's hesitation, Nika followed him.

The bear glanced at Nika. Ruth saw that it was a very cool glance, with a warning in it.

Nika understood something of the bear's glance too. She sensed that the bear did not like what she was doing. She hesitated again, but then with her head held high, she stepped forward firmly, though she trembled inside.

She had come to think of Tek as her grandfather — her old and ailing grandfather. And she was *not* going to let her grandfather approach this powerful bear alone. She would accompany her dying grandfather, whether this bear liked it or not.

She followed Tek up to the doorway and stood by his side before the bear.

This was definitely *not* what the bear wanted. The bear's eyes were angry, and haughty, and the bear made several deep grunts that ruffled Tek's fur and Nika's hair.

Nika looked up at the bear, as steadily as possible. She tried to keep her expression neutral. She would not plead for acceptance. She would not show her own anger which flared from the bear's quick judgment of her, that she was valueless.

The bear turned his gaze from her, dismissively, and looked down at Tek. Then he backed away from the door frame, enough for Tek to move forward to stand before him, outside of the house.

Tek crossed the door's threshold.

Nika did too.

The bear brought his nose down and sniffed Tek all over, finishing with the loop of hide strips around Tek's neck, that held the flint pieces. The sniff–over was long, and thorough. Throughout it, the bear completely ignored Nika.

When he was finished sniffing Tek, the bear raised his head, and suddenly his paw swept around Tek. In a blink he had gathered Tek to his chest, turned and disappeared into the fog.

But Nika had sensed it coming. She had seen it in the bear's eyes as his nose marauded over Tek. This bear was going to take Tek away, and he was going to do it very soon, and very quickly.

She was shapeshifting to owl before the bear had finished raising his head. She had her talons in the braided hide strips of Tek's loose collar before the bear had his paw fully around Tek. She was swept up into the fur of the bear's chest with Tek, close to the bear's booming heart as he carried her and Tek away with him.

* * *

The dog gave a woof of surprise and went to the open door, but did not go outside. Within seconds the rain returned in force, with strong winds and a heavily rumbling thunder.

Ruth closed the door against the blowing rain. At first she was not sure whether to latch it, in case Nika came right back, but then she did latch it. Nika was obviously determined to go wherever the lynx went. She might eventually come back, but if she did, it probably would not happen this night.

Ruth had stood near the doorway while the bear was sniffing Tek all over. When he was nearly through with that, he threw a glance Ruth's way. She did not quite understand it until after the bear had left, taking Tek and Nika with him. Then she understood. It was over. The bear did not intend to ever come back here, at least not in her lifetime. And since he had come here for Tek, Tek would not be coming back either.

As for Nika . . . Ruth was not sure whether Nika would find her way back here, but if she did, it would probably take her some time to do it. At *least* a week or so. And, as had happened to Ruth when she had travelled with the bear as a child, time was bound to move strangely for Nika while she was gone.

* * *

Nika never did return, at least not to Ruth's knowledge, in her lifetime.

The girl was truly missed by Phoebe and Ruth. She had not been with them for very long, but she had cast a warm glow, much stronger than seemed possible to have come from her slight form.

171

They had loved her dearly, trusted her implicitly, and appreciated everything she had done to help them, and to save them.

In their moment of most desperate need, during Carrie and Sedric's attack, she had found them in the dark and rallied them. At every turn after that she was there in the thick of it, wresting victory for them from certain defeat.

Over the years they thought of Nika often, and whenever they happened to see a small owl flying silently through the sky at dawn or dusk. They thought of her and wondered where she was, what she was doing, and if she was happy. One thing they were certain of. Wherever she was, she was a force for good, in the battles of life. For that was her nature. That was her soul.

End Book Two